Chasing Rayna

SYLVIA NOBEL

Read & enjoy !

Nite Owl
Books

Phoenix,
Arizona

Phoenix,
Arizona

Copyright © 2004 by Sylvia Nobel

For information, contact Nite Owl Books
4040 E. Camelback Road, #101
Phoenix, Arizona 85018-2736
(602) 840-0132
1-888-927-9600
FAX (602) 957-1671
e-mail: theniteowl@juno.com
www.niteowlbooks.com

ISBN 0-9661105-4-4

Cover Design by
ATG Productions
Christy A. Moeller – Phoenix, Arizona

Library of Congress Control Number: 2003113881

TO MY WONDERFUL
FAMILY AND FRIENDS
THANK YOU FOR YOUR
LOVE, PATIENCE AND
ENCOURAGEMENT

ACKNOWLEDGMENTS

*****

The author wishes to acknowledge the
invaluable assistance of the following people:

Madeline Hendricks, Prosecutor
Tina Williams, Editorial Services
Donna Jandro, Editorial Services
Brandon Williams, Computer Consulting
Chris Lovelace, Systems Engineer
Kelly Scott-Olson and Christy A. Moeller,
ATG Productions, Phoenix, AZ

CHAPTER ONE

Rayna Manchester paused in the doorway of the cluttered office she shared with Deputy Prosecutor Miguel Castillo, meeting his startled gaze as he cradled the phone. "Hey, look who's here! I didn't expect you back until next week," he crowed, his brown eyes twinkling with good humor. "Please tell me you had a good time. And I hope you kicked back and relaxed for once in your life."

"I did." No point in mentioning the disquieting dream that she'd had again, or that the sound of her own sobs had awakened her. She'd felt confident that after all these years, she'd finally grown beyond it, that the heartaches clouding her past could touch her no longer.

He cocked his head to one side. "You had another week's vacation coming. Why didn't you take it?"

She slid into the leather chair behind her desk. "You know me," she replied, glancing out the window at the morning rush hour traffic crawling through the streets of downtown Tucson, "I needed the break, but I'm happier when I'm in the thick of things."

His knowing grin disputed her response. "I see. So, you're all recovered from losing the Stratton case?"

She edged him a rueful look. "Believe me, I tried to put it out of my mind."

His steady gaze remained thoughtful. "There's no question you worked your fanny off on that one. You should have won it."

Yes, she should have. She tried not to think of the countless hours she'd invested, only to lose the case on a minor technicality. During the sensational trial, the State had introduced more than enough evidence for a conviction, but much to her chagrin, the guilty party, a loathsome man who'd allegedly strangled his own mother and dumped her body into his recycle bin, had walked out free as a bird. And all because a law clerk had failed to file one important document which the defense attorney had gleefully waved in her face—one lousy little piece of paper. Nevertheless, she still blamed herself for the fact that justice had not been served. To her added embarrassment, she'd been raked over the coals, perhaps skewered was a more appropriate term, by every radio talk show host in town. The print press also had a field day headlining that, after four years, Pima County Deputy Prosecutor Rayna Manchester's perfect record of convictions had finally been broken. Remembering the gallons of midnight oil she'd burned on that one case galled her to no end.

"Great tan," Miguel said with an admiring grin. "So, where'd you go skiing again? Aspen? Vail?"

She made a face at him. "Sure. Like I could afford those places on my salary."

"You will someday. You're gaining quite a reputation and I expect one of the big firms to snap you up any day now." He leaned down, dug a newspaper from the stack on the floor beside his desk, and held it aloft. "Did you know about this?"

Rayna adjusted the clasp that gathered her dark, shoulder-length hair at the nape of her neck and eyed the bold headline. MOM AND TODDLER FIGHT FOR LIVES AFTER DEADLY HIT AND RUN.

"I read about it after I left. Have the police got a suspect?"

"Yeah. An eighteen-year-old kid turned himself in a couple of days later. Apparently he'd only been in town a week or two when it happened. He claimed he'd been too scared to come forward and say anything until the description of his vehicle was all over the news."

Rayna's interest level shot up and she felt the familiar tingle in her belly. This could be big, considering the victims were the sister and two-year-old niece of Tucson's popular mayor. "What are the charges?"

"Two counts of Aggravated Assault with a Dangerous Instrument and one count of Leaving the Scene."

"Who did Mitchell assign to the case?"

"No one, yet. And believe me, if my case load weren't up to here," he said, pushing the back of his hand beneath his chin for emphasis, "I wouldn't mind taking a stab at this one myself. I handled the Initial Appearance last Wednesday and it made me sick. Damned pimply-faced punk didn't show even a smidgen of remorse. And wouldn't you know it, the kid's rich daddy flew into town and posted bond." His face darkened. "It burns me up knowing that the two of them are living high on the hog over at the Marriott while that woman and her baby are lying...."

"Welcome back." Mitchell Gates's gravelly voice boomed from the doorway. "Ready to hit the bricks?"

Rayna turned to see her craggy-faced boss resting his towering bulk against the doorframe while he extended a folder in her direction. "Add whatever you have to this stack," she said, patting the pile on her desk. "You know I'm a glutton for punishment."

"We'll clear some of the other things from your calendar. Right now, I want you to concentrate on this hit-

3

and-run," he said, dropping the folder in front of her. "I guess I don't need to tell you that there is a considerable amount of pressure from above on this one."

"All right!" Rayna exclaimed, relishing the challenge. Mitchell was well aware of how hard she'd taken the loss of the previous case. She tapped her fingers on the folder and threw him a grateful smile. "Miguel was just filling me in."

His hazel eyes took on a crafty gleam. "Did Miguel also tell you who's handling the defense?"

"No," she said, slowly drawing the word out, her quizzical gaze moving from one to the other. "But, the Cheshire cat grins you're both wearing gives me a pretty good idea."

Mitchell shoved his hands into the pockets of his baggy slacks and laughed out loud. "Go for the gold. Freestone won't know what hit him."

***

The first day back at work behind her, Rayna stopped at the gym on the way home. She could have easily done without more exercise since her muscles still ached from skiing, but she needed it nonetheless. She didn't work out five times a week just to stay in shape. It was balm for her soul, the ideal prescription to relieve stress after a twelve-hour day.

After an hour of step aerobics and a half hour of spinning, Rayna showered and changed into a loose sweatshirt and leggings before strolling across the strip mall towards the juice bar, inhaling deep breaths of crisp night air, finally feeling relaxed. She loved winters in Arizona, when the searing heat of summer finally relinquished its iron grip. Once indoors again, Rayna quickly snagged two stools at the crowded counter and ordered a drink. The snippets of animated conversation from the other patrons, mingled with occasional bursts of laughter, created a welcome change from the somber atmosphere of the courtroom. A light slap on her shoulder caused her to jump, and she turned to meet Tracy Butler's luminous green eyes.

"Hey, girlfriend, you missed out on all the excitement at the zoo last Saturday," her friend announced, dropping her backpack at her feet as she eased onto the adjacent stool.

"Don't tell me the white tiger had her cub?"

"She did! But that's not the half of it. While the TV crews and newspaper reporters were all concentrating on the cub, one of the spectators went into labor right there on the spot. It was crazy! We called the fire department and not two minutes later the lady delivered a seven-pound baby girl. The reporters went ballistic trying to cover both stories at once."

Rayna shook her head in wonder. "Go figure. I've been volunteering there for nearly three years and the most exciting thing that's ever happened on my shift was some kid locking himself in the bathroom."

"That'll teach you to take a vacation." Tracy giggled, waving to the dark-haired man behind the counter. "Hey, Brian, I'll take one of your special strawberry smoothies when you get a minute."

He winked at her. "Right away."

Tracy sighed happily and whispered, "He's kinda hot, isn't he?"

Rayna studied the young man's buff body and pleasing profile. "Kinda."

"Speaking of hot," Tracy began, her eyes sparkling with mischief, "how did you and Gary hit it off the other night?"

Rayna gave her friend a sidelong glance. "Hmm. Interesting segue." She pretended to concentrate on her coconut-pineapple smoothie for long seconds before answering. "He was nice."

"Nice? Just nice?" Tracy squeaked in disbelief. "He's young, not exactly a hottie, but not bad-looking either, he has a successful dental practice, drives a new red Porsche, probably has a fat bank account...and that's all you can say?"

"Young is the operative word."

Tracy grimaced, tucking a strand of wispy red hair behind one ear. "You're not robbing the cradle. After all, he's at least thirty, and you're what, not quite thirty-five? Lighten up, woman, it's the cool thing to do nowadays."

"For Hollywood stars maybe."

Tracy flashed Brian a coy smile and thanked him for her drink before returning her attention to Rayna. "So, what about Kevin and me? He's four years younger and it doesn't matter one bit. So, what's the *real* excuse this time? Are you going to give Gary the brush-off like the last two guys I've sent your way?"

Rayna appreciated her friend's well-meaning efforts, but Gary had sparked no fireworks. Zilch. "Before I left for vacation, I promised him we'd get together again when I got back from vacation this week. Happy?"

Tracy solemnly clinked her glass to Rayna's in obvious approval. "Happy."

It was closing in on nine o'clock by the time Rayna reached her condo, bone tired, but content to be back at work. Her mind was still humming with details of the hectic afternoon as she walked into the lobby and retrieved her mail from the row of brass boxes along the back wall. Normally, she would have taken the stairs, but tonight she stepped into the elevator, piling the handful of envelopes on top of the files and work clothes nestled in the crook of her arm before punching the button for the third floor.

Dinner first, she told herself firmly. Then she'd dig into the material on the new case. She'd been so swamped all day with court appearances, returning phone calls and tackling the mounds of paperwork on her desk, that she'd never had time to even glance at the folder.

The elevator door slid open and she hurried along the carpeted hallway, head down, rummaging in her purse for her keys. She looked up just in time to avoid colliding with her neighbor, who'd stepped suddenly from her doorway.

"Oh!" Rayna cried, reaching out to steady the frail woman wearing a flowered housecoat. "I'm sorry Mrs. Ansel, I guess I wasn't paying attention."

"No harm done," the woman said with a hesitant smile. "Did you have a good day back at the office?"

Rayna cringed at the expectant gleam in the old woman's watery-blue eyes. She had neither the time, nor was she in the mood, to get trapped in an extended conversation.

"I did." She brushed past and slid the key into the lock before pausing. She hadn't meant to sound so abrupt. Margaret Ansel was kind and considerate, her only shortcoming being that she was usually starved for company. Besides, who else could she trust to take care of Beauregarde when she was away? Rayna turned back and sweetened her tone. "I'd ask you in to visit, but I have a ton of work to catch up on tonight."

"Oh, that's quite all right," Mrs. Ansel said, nervously picking non-existent lint from her housecoat in a transparent attempt to hide her disappointment. "I don't have time to talk anyway. My program starts in a few minutes. I just wanted to remind you that the carpet cleaners are coming this Friday in case you want to bring Beauregarde over while they're shampooing your place."

"Oh, I completely forgot."

"Just bring his litter box and a couple of cans of his favorite food and we'll have a grand time together."

"You're a lifesaver, Mrs. Ansel. Thank you." Rayna flashed her an appreciative smile, pushed the door open and locked it behind her. She snapped on the light and her eyes instantly focused on the six-foot-tall rubber plant lying prone on the living room floor. "Oh, Beauregarde, not again." She shook her head at the large white cat staring back at her from the couch, his cornflower blue eyes brimming with innocence. "And don't give me that I-didn't-do-it look." She set the files on the cluttered antique library table before kneeling to push the plant upright. While dismayed at the damp potting soil scattered on the cream-colored carpet, she consoled herself with the fact that it would soon be cleaned.

She slipped off her jacket and gazed around the airy room, enveloped by a warm glow of satisfaction at her recent purchase. The bold-print throw covers recommended by the store designer had worked beautifully to unify her mismatched antique furniture collection. The oval mirror she'd found last week at the thrift store would finish off the décor nicely.

Beauregarde landed on the floor with a soft thud and approached her, meowing softly, his tail waving languidly as he weaved in and out between her legs.

8

"Don't try to sweet talk me," she scolded mildly, scooping him into her arms. She stroked his silky fur and the cat nuzzled her neck before wriggling from her arms to stand by his empty food bowl. "And I suppose you now expect me to reward your shenanigans with dinner," she said with a chuckle, striding past the breakfast bar into the narrow kitchen. The red light on the answering machine flashed, so she tapped the button. As the tape rewound, she opened a can of cat food and poured it into Beauregarde's bowl. She listened to three hang-ups and two sales calls before a genial voice resonated, "Hey there, it's Gary. I hope the skiing was good. Listen, I was wondering if you'd like to see a play with me Saturday night. It's the premiere of 'Corridors,' that off-Broadway show I mentioned, and we could catch an early dinner beforehand. Give me a call if this will work for you."

She kicked off her shoes and stood at the counter, lost in thought, absently watching Beauregarde daintily chew his food. The New York critics had given the play great reviews. Unfortunately, she couldn't muster up any enthusiasm at the thought of seeing it with Gary Sykes. Besides, she'd probably be too busy. Of course she'd be too busy. She'd make damn sure of that. Tracy was right. She'd become a veritable pro at keeping potential suitors at arm's length, a seasoned master at conjuring up convenient excuses whenever a man showed the slightest interest in her. And she knew why.

Her eyes glazed over as fragments of the sensual dream danced in her head, resurrecting conflicting emotions of desire and resentment followed by a crushing sense of loss. Would she ever again meet a man capable of igniting the magnitude of passion that had once consumed her? Lord knows she'd made every effort to forget him

9

after her well-intentioned marriage to Thomas Manchester, who had been the kindest, most patient husband a woman could wish for. But it seemed no matter what she did, no matter how far she ran she was incapable of purging the memories and there remained an indefinable yearning in the deepest recesses of her heart.

With a sigh of annoyance, Rayna grabbed the remote, turned on the TV and concentrated on dinner preparations. It was routine by now. Whenever her thoughts led her to the dangerous precipice overlooking her past and threatened to send her on a downward spiral of depression, her natural defense mechanism would kick in and firmly close the door to the bittersweet memories.

An hour later, clad in her white bathrobe and fuzzy slippers, Rayna settled onto the sofa with the file on her lap and Beauregarde curled beside her, his rumbling purr filling the silence as she scratched his head and flipped the folder open to study the accident report. Then she scanned the witness statement and the notes Miguel had penned during the Initial Appearance.

She'd prosecuted numerous DUIs during her career, and dealing with the disastrous consequences of drunk driving cases had hardened her to life's cruel realities. But, as she reviewed the grim details and the extent of the injuries sustained by these victims, the usual objectivity for which she prided herself gradually dissipated. Her face grew hot with anger. How could anyone be so callous, so utterly heartless as to run down a mother and child in a marked crosswalk and then make no attempt to stop or render aid? Her throat tightened as she reviewed the photos of the woman and the little girl. Abruptly, she set them aside, refusing to become emotionally involved.

The preliminary hearing was scheduled for Wednesday. That gave her very little time to prepare. She scribbled a few notes on a yellow legal pad. First thing tomorrow she would contact the investigating officer and the eyewitness to arrange interviews and make sure they would be available to appear in court.

Flipping the page, her gaze zeroed in on the name of the defendant: Scott Brockwell, age eighteen. She stared at it, her hand suspended in mid-air, her stomach turning cold. Brockwell? What were the chances? No, she told herself firmly. This was a coincidence. There had to be literally hundreds of people with that same last name. She tried to shake it off, but the indelible memory began to replay in her mind. She'd been only sixteen the day Tyler Brockwell walked into the little photo shop where she worked, and into her young life—altering it forever.

***

Rayna pushed against the tall wooden door and stepped inside the courtroom, feeling confidently prepared for the preliminary hearing. Involuntarily, her eyes swept over the people sitting in the gallery. When she saw no recognizable faces, her sense of relief was extreme. She took her place at the narrow wooden table assigned to the prosecution and sifted through her notes, wishing she hadn't left her suit jacket upstairs in the office. It was always cold and drafty in this particular courtroom.

She pretended not to notice when Sheldon Freestone arrived, accompanied by his teenage client. Displaying his habitual fanfare, he dropped his overstuffed briefcase onto the defense table with a loud bang then grunted while he removed his jacket and tossed it over the back of his chair while motioning for the young man to take a seat beside him.

Rayna raised her head to meet the seasoned attorney's heavy-lidded gaze and masked her disgust at the sight of his shirt buttons straining across his ample stomach.

He puffed out his chest importantly and ambled towards her. "Always such a pleasure, Ms. Manchester."

"Good morning," she said, answering his patronizing tone with forced courtesy.

"No hard feelings about the Stratton case, I hope."

"None whatsoever."

"You win some, you lose some."

She concealed her irritation at his insincere display of concern. Freestone's arrogant smirk was interrupted by the clerk's announcement, "All rise," as the judge swept into the room, took his seat and advised everyone to sit down. He adjusted the sleeves of his black robe and donned reading glasses before announcing the day's date followed by, "CR 783091, State of Arizona versus Scott Brockwell. This is the time set for a preliminary hearing. Please note your appearances for the record. Are you ready to proceed?"

"Yes, Your Honor," she said, rising to her feet. "Rayna Manchester on behalf of the State."

"Sheldon Freestone representing Scott Brockwell, Your Honor."

The judge asked, "Is Mr. Brockwell present?"

"Yes, Your Honor," Freestone replied, leaning to whisper something to the longhaired adolescent.

"Your Honor," Rayna began, "the State calls Officer Lyle Harris to the stand."

As soon as the uniformed officer had been sworn in and stated his name for the record, she established that he was a patrol officer, employed by the city of Tucson, Arizona, before continuing with, "Were you so employed at 9:30 p.m. on the night of January tenth of this year?"

"Yes," he replied, settling himself comfortably in the chair.

"Were you in the vicinity of Oracle and Sunrise Lane?"

"Yes."

Rayna prompted him to recount his recollections of the night in question and he explained how he'd arrived at the scene to first see the mangled stroller and then the victims lying in the street.

"Can you describe their condition?"

"They were really messed up. I could see there was a lot of trauma...."

Freestone shouted, "Objection. He's not a medical doctor."

The judge peered at Rayna over the top of his glasses. "Can you lay more foundation, Counselor?"

"Could you state the nature of the injuries as you observed them, Officer Harris?" She noted with satisfaction that his impassive expression dissolved to one of distress. "Both the woman and the baby were bleeding pretty bad, there were facial lacerations...um...I could tell by the angle of the woman's right leg that it was probably broken. The little girl was whimpering, obviously she was in a lot of pain..." His emotional pause intensified the hush in the courtroom. "I accompanied the victims to the hospital after the ambulance arrived."

Rayna glanced at her notes. "Did you speak to the physician who treated the injuries that same night?"

"I did."

"And have you spoken with him since that night?"

"Yes," he answered, shifting in his seat. "This morning."

"What did the doctor say about their condition?"

"He said they're both still in extremely critical condition. The woman is suffering from internal injuries, her right leg is broken in several places...the daughter has extensive head injuries, a fractured shoulder and other complications."

"Will the doctor be available to testify should this come to trial?"

"Yes."

"No more questions at this time," Rayna said, turning to take her seat.

When Freestone's subsequent cross-examination produced no significant challenge, she called the middle-aged woman who was the sole witness to the accident. "Please describe what you saw that night," Rayna prompted her after she'd been sworn in.

The woman cleared her throat nervously. "Like I told the officer, I'd just finished shopping and had turned west onto Sunrise to head home."

"Is that a two-way street?"

"Yes, Ma'am."

"Continue."

"I guess I'd only driven a couple of hundred yards when I noticed a lady with a stroller standing on the sidewalk."

"Was she on the left or right hand side of the road?"

"The left."

"Did you stop?"

"Yes."

"Was there a clearly marked crosswalk?"

"Yes."

"And what happened next?"

"I waved for her to go ahead and cross. She smiled and waved back at me, I guess to say thanks, and she was walking right in front of my car when I looked in my rear-view mirror and saw these headlights barreling down on me." At that point, the woman's face grew flushed. "I swear, I thought the car was going to crash into the back of mine...but then, at the last second, it swung around me...."

Rayna interjected, "Can you describe the vehicle?"

"Yes. It was a green SUV with what looked like orange flames or something painted on the side."

"Thank you, proceed."

"Well, anyway, it suddenly swerved around me on the right side, weaving all over the place and then...just..." she paused, lips trembling, and there was a distinct tremor in her voice when she concluded, "mowed them down. It was horrible, the most horrible thing I've ever seen in my life."

Rayna stole a glance at the baby-faced defendant. Lazily chewing gum, his expression bland, he exhibited no remorse and that bothered her. She suppressed a flare of irritation and returned her attention to the witness. "So, the mother and child were crossing from the south side of the street to the north side, is that correct?"

"Yes."

"Did you see the driver of the SUV?"

"Yeah, the window on the driver's side was open and I clearly saw his blonde hair blowing in the wind."

"Do you see that person today?"

Her eyes narrowed in disgust as she pointed to Scott Brockwell. "That's him."

"May the record reflect identification of the defendant," Rayna said, addressing the bench, then asked the woman, "What happened next?"

"A guy came running out from the parking lot and called 911 on his cell phone. I got out to see if I could help. They were just lying there...I thought they were dead." She covered her face with both hands and when she lowered them, tears glimmered in her eyes. "I was afraid to touch them because I heard you're not supposed to in case they might have a head or neck injury."

"Did the driver of the vehicle return to render aid?"

The woman's mouth tightened as she glared at Scott Brockwell. "No, Ma'am. He kept on driving and never came back."

Satisfied with the witness's responses, Rayna concluded and returned to her seat as Freestone shrugged into his shapeless jacket and approached the stand. "You said the vehicle tore around you," he said, dramatically punching his fist through the air. "Did you have any way to clock how fast it was going?"

She looked uncomfortable. "Well...no, but I'd say he was going every bit of fifty miles an hour. Maybe more."

"Isn't it possible that the driver of the SUV was forced to swerve to avoid hitting you when you stopped so abruptly? In other words, *you* could have caused the accident by stopping for no apparent reason."

Rayna called out, "Objection. Calls for conclusion."

"Sustained," intoned the judge.

Freestone continued, "In your statement you said the driver was weaving and appeared under the influence.

How did you know this? Did you administer a breathalyzer test on the spot?"

Her face blanched. "Well, no, but he must have been tanked. He practically ran into a phone pole when he turned the corner."

"Thank you, that will be all."

Rayna nodded her approval to the obviously shaken woman as she stepped down and hurried past her table. As the judge studied something in his folder, she noticed Scott Brockwell staring over his shoulder into gallery behind them. Was she imagining it, or did she detect a gleam of distress mirrored in his deep-set blue eyes? Was he shaking his head ever so slightly? At that instant, he realized Rayna was looking at him and quickly averted his gaze. Puzzled by his surreptitious behavior, Rayna turned to scan the crowded gallery, filled with citizens of all races, ages, and in all manner of dress. Taking his agitated expression into consideration, Rayna concentrated on the younger people. Which one of the sullen-faced young women had he been trying to communicate with—the teenage girl with orange and green hair, or the pretty brunette with the nose and eyebrow rings? Or was it the slender young woman with long blonde hair wearing a wide-brimmed hat that shadowed half of her face? As Rayna's gaze drifted from person to person, her eyes locked onto one particular man seated in the second row. All at once, it seemed as if all the air had been pumped from the room and a strange numbness clutched her. In utter disbelief, she stared at the much older, but very familiar face of Tyler Brockwell.

CHAPTER TWO

Tyler sat thunderstruck, scarcely able to fathom the ironic circumstances that had brought him to Arizona to face Rayna after nineteen years. With her own reaction confirming the realization that had slowly dawned on him the past half hour, he stared back at her, his pulse hammering with the final shock of recognition.

"That's the prosecuting attorney," Sheldon Freestone had whispered to him when they'd first stepped into the courtroom. "She's a real bulldog. We have our work cut out for us," he'd added begrudgingly.

Never in a million years would Tyler have imagined that the woman with dark wavy hair would turn out to be Rayna Daniels from Summersville, South Carolina. But there'd been something about her right from the start. Perhaps it was her voice and the faint remains of long southern vowels. Then there was the familiar tilt of her chin when he'd glimpsed her profile. Yes, she was the right height, he'd acknowledged, his blood rushing as he sized up the petite figure. He edged forward for a better look. For the greater part of his life, he'd guarded in a special corner of his heart the memory of that sixteen-year old beauty, his first and only love. It was not until he'd stared into those unforgettable violet eyes that he'd been absolutely sure. It was a moment charged with an emotion more powerful than anything he'd experienced in his entire adult life.

An exclamation of surprise lodged in Rayna's throat as she turned away. The intense look she'd just exchanged with Tyler made her feel as though she'd been suspended in time. She wrestled with emotions so diverse, so profound, she dared not attempt to identify them. It was a mighty struggle just to maintain calm.

What were the odds, she mused incredulously, that of all the people on the face of the earth, she'd find him here in a Tucson courtroom, associated with her case, possibly the father of the very person she was attempting to convict? How well she remembered those expressive brown eyes, the way they would sparkle when he laughed and the power they'd had to melt away her resistance. Oh, God! She had to be out of her mind to be inviting these thoughts now. No, she couldn't allow herself to view this stranger as the Tyler Brockwell she had spent the majority of her life trying to forget.

She tried to dismiss him from her mind and concentrate on the report in front of her. But his face supplanted the words on the page, a face she'd known only too well. He looked very much the same except for the determined lines around his mouth and the slightest touch of gray highlighting his thick brown hair. Even with her back to him, she was acutely aware of his eyes on her. She desperately wanted to believe that she had made a mistake, that her eyes had deceived her, that she was simply imagining him there. But she could not bring herself to turn around a second time to verify her suspicion. The truth was she knew full well that he was no figment of her imagination.

While trying to get his bearings after the shock of seeing Rayna, Tyler noticed Sheldon Freestone signaling him to approach the barrier. He rose and moved forward to meet him.

"I did the best I could to discredit the witness's testimony," Freestone whispered, "but I don't think the judge is buying it. At this point it's unlikely there will be a dismissal. We'll have an opportunity to plead these charges down, but if not, you'd best brace yourself for trial."

Tyler squared his jaw. "Give it to me straight. What are my son's chances?"

"Hard to tell at this juncture, too many variables. But I'll give it my best shot."

Tyler returned to his seat, disheartened by Sheldon's less-than-encouraging statement. The possibility that his son could be sentenced to prison left him feeling hollow. He was convinced that, to some degree, the unfortunate incident was his fault. Would Scott have left home three weeks ago, without a word, if they'd had a good relationship and better communication?

After receiving the unexpected call for help ten days ago, he'd rushed to his son's side, hoping against hope that they could begin to mend their tenuous relationship. Instead, his presence had spawned only guarded arguments and icy recriminations between them. Tyler felt more alienated from Scott's affections than ever and fervently wished things had been different. And now, Rayna's unforeseen role in this predicament added a unique and astonishing dimension.

Rayna sat stiffly, wishing she could somehow make herself invisible. She expelled a sigh of relief when the judge finally announced that he had found probable cause that a crime had been committed. He affirmed the current release conditions and ruled that the case be bound over to Superior Court for trial, setting the date for April 9th. He had barely rendered his decision when she began collecting her files and jamming them into her briefcase. Poised to make a speedy exit from the courtroom, she turned to leave, but was intercepted by Donna Platt, a defense attorney she would face in court later that same afternoon.

Huddled with Scott near the side door, Tyler summoned his concentration as he listened to Freestone explain the ramifications of the judge's decision and outline the legal strategy he felt they should pursue. Involuntarily, his gaze strayed in Rayna's direction as she stood with her back to him conversing with another woman.

"Hey, listen, I gotta scram," Scott announced, eyeing his watch as he backed away. "They're kinda shorthanded at the restaurant today." He nodded curtly in his father's direction. "Catch you later."

Out of the corner of his eye, Tyler noticed that Rayna had concluded her conversation and was now heading towards the door. The compelling need to speak to her suddenly took precedence over everything else. "Ah...thanks, Sheldon," he said in a distracted tone, hastily pumping Freestone's hand. "I have to make a few phone calls myself."

"Wait a minute. We have a lot more to discuss," Freestone countered with a disapproving frown.

"That we do," Tyler concurred, watching the door swing shut behind Rayna. "I will a...I'll call you later." Judging by the bemused expression on Freestone's face, he knew his behavior must seem odd indeed. But he couldn't help it. Fate had brought him together again with Rayna and there was no force on earth capable of keeping him away from her. He rushed out the door and paused in the marble hallway, his eyes searching the corridor until he spotted her at the far end stepping onto an escalator. By God, she'd moved fast! Seeing how she'd swept out of the courtroom without so much as a glance in his direction, he was certain she was attempting to evade him. He broke into a run, shouting, "Rayna, wait!"

The nape of her neck tingled when she heard the sound of his voice behind her. Gripped by an unreasonable sense of cold panic, she hurried up the last few steps, almost tripping in her haste, and made a beeline for her office.

Tyler bounded up the escalator three steps at a time, overtaking several startled riders. Determined, and more than a little annoyed at her attempt to elude him, he ran faster. After all these years, after all he'd been through, she damned well owed him an explanation.

Rayna's sense of relief was short-lived. Just as she reached for the door, she felt his hand on her arm. She whirled to face him. "Take your hands off me."

"What was the point of that steeple chase?" he panted, quickly releasing her. "Why the hell are you acting like you don't know who I am?"

"I'd appreciate it if you'd speak to me in a civil tone." She fought to sustain a façade of indifference.

"I'm sorry," he said, softening his tone. "I...I need to talk with you."

She gave him a hard look. "To be honest, I wouldn't know what to say to you."

"Hello would be a good start."

"Goodbye is better."

"Five minutes is all I ask."

"I can't. It's unethical. Am I right to assume that Scott Brockwell is your son?"

Tyler flinched, taken aback by her harsh tone. "Yes, he's my son, but what I have to say doesn't concern him. It concerns us."

"Us? There is no *us* and hasn't been for…for…light years! Now if you'll excuse me, I have a lot of work to do." She started to open the door to the reception area, but he moved to block her escape. "Wait just a minute. I have about a thousand questions that need answers."

Rayna wondered if her face was as red as it felt. "About what?"

"About you. About what happened after that…last night we were together."

"That was then, this is now," Rayna replied, her tone clipped and unemotional. "Whatever transpired between us no longer matters so let it go. I have." Sidestepping him, she pulled the door open, thinking to herself, *what a flat-out liar you are!*

He followed her inside. "Well, I haven't. Damn it, Rayna, you owe me an explanation."

The steely-eyed receptionist shot her a look of alarm. "Is there something wrong, Ms. Manchester? Shall I call security?"

Rayna hastened to soothe her. "That won't be necessary, Tammy. The gentleman is leaving." She warned him away with her eyes.

Ms. Manchester? For the first time, he noticed that she wore no wedding ring.

Noting the flare of anticipation lighting his face, Rayna feared her resolve would weaken. "Goodbye, Mr. Brockwell." Without a backward glance, she marched into her office.

Tyler stood still for a moment, feeling self-conscious and more than a little foolish as the receptionist eyed him with suspicion through the glass partition. He flashed her a sheepish grin and withdrew into the hallway. Rayna couldn't avoid him forever. She'd have to leave her office sometime. So, he'd wait. He pulled out his cell phone and sat down on a nearby bench where he was partially concealed by a large potted plant. Good. He had a clear view of her office door without being immediately visible to her.

Reaching the sanctuary of her office, Rayna wasn't sure her trembling knees would support her as she swept past Miguel's desk and sank into the chair, her mind swirling in bewildered astonishment.

"¡Dios mio!" Miguel exclaimed, staring at her. "You look as white as flour. Don't tell me Freestone's got you riled up already?"

"It's not Freestone," she answered weakly.

"Oh? So it's not the Brockwell case?"

"It is the Brockwell case. Damn it!" She hadn't meant to raise her voice, but her stress level was heading through the roof.

Miguel drew back, perplexed. "Well, hell, that explains everything."

Rayna edged him an apologetic smile. "I'm sorry. I'm not making any sense, am I?"

"Not really." He pushed aside a stack of files and leaned forward on his elbows. "You want to talk about it?"

She looked away from him and began to shuffle through the pile of papers crowding her desk. "No."

"It might help," he prodded gently.

"Maybe, maybe not."

"Look, I'm already late for a deposition, but what do you say I buy you lunch afterwards?"

She eyed him hesitantly.

"Come on, meet me in the cafeteria. One hour tops."

Rayna met the calm, nonjudgmental look in his dark eyes and nodded. As she had done so many times before, she thanked God for Miguel Castillo's friendship.

***

Tyler was on his fourth call and deep in conversation when he looked up from his notepad and realized Rayna was among the throng of people moving past him towards the escalator. She hadn't noticed him. "Don...Don, listen...no, I can't make a decision about that right now. Can I call you later? Good." He flipped the phone shut, jumped up and had to stop himself from breaking into a run. When he reached the bottom of the escalator his heart sank. She didn't appear to be anywhere around. How had she disappeared so quickly? Halfway out of the building, he stopped, suddenly aware of the appetizing aroma of hot food. Turning, he made his way back inside, looking for the source, and then followed a trio of cheerfully chattering women as they rushed through a doorway leading to a small cafeteria. He paused and scanned the noisy lunch crowd, feeling a wave of relief wash over him when he spotted Rayna sitting alone at a corner table. The passing years had not detracted from her startling good looks. If anything, she'd grown even more beautiful. He squared his shoulders as if to gear himself for battle, then marched purposefully towards her.

As though drawn by some inexplicable force, Rayna looked up from her brief and drew in a sharp breath as she watched Tyler stride towards her. Before she could determine her feelings, decide on what action to take, or formulate any words, he sat down and fastened her with a commanding look that invited no argument.

"The way I see it, you have two choices. We can either sit here and talk quietly like mature adults, or you can get up and try to run away from me again, in which case I'll follow until you agree to listen to me."

"I don't think I care for either option," she said flatly. "I'm meeting someone for lunch. Please leave." She pretended to study the folder in front of her, but the words blurred together and made no sense.

Tyler ignored her request. "I always wondered whether I'd ever see you again, but I never dreamed it would be under these circumstances." She looked so incredibly desirable it was an effort not to touch her. *Whoa!* He cautioned himself. *Don't screw this up.* After a few seconds of awkward silence, he leaned back and folded his arms. "It appears that the years have been more than agreeable to you since we last saw each other. I mean your career and everything," he said, choosing his words judiciously. How could he tell her what he was really thinking?

"Yes, I have my life very well in order, thank you," she replied, making eye contact with him, hoping her cool tone masked her erratic pulse rate.

"Good for you. I'm happy to hear that," he snapped, unable to conceal his bitterness. "Obviously you didn't have the slightest concern about *my* life after you ran out on me."

"I think you have it out of sequence," she countered, sudden fury lighting her violet eyes. "Apparently, you've forgotten that it was you who got engaged...to...what's her name one day after promising me..." She waved one hand impatiently. "It's not important."

"It is important. That's not how it happened."

"Did you or did you not get engaged the very next day?" she asked with icy reproach.

Her tone saddened him. It was as though she were interrogating a criminal in court. "Not right away, not the way you think. Why wouldn't you return my phone calls or answer any of my letters? Why didn't you give me the chance to explain what happened?"

"Explain what? That you were seeing someone else at the same time you were dangling me on a string?" Rayna was amazed at the level of anger she still harbored.

"Look, I will admit to you that I already knew Camille, but I wasn't dating her. Not after I met you. Not after we...got close." He searched her eyes. "Rayna, did I miss something? I thought we shared something very special."

She gave him a level stare. "So did I."

"Then why did you do it? Just sneak off into the night and marry that...that Manchester fellow?" he exclaimed, his voice rising. "Christ, wasn't he at least ten or fifteen years older than you were?"

She looked around to make sure they had not attracted the attention of the other diners before turning back to confront him. "If you must know, I married someone who wanted and respected me, someone who accepted me for who I was. He didn't judge me because I didn't belong to the country club set like you and your hateful family." She hadn't meant to sound so indignant and experienced a twinge of surprise when the smoldering accusation in his eyes turned to melancholy. How could she ever tell him the real reason that compelled her to marry Thomas Manchester? Miguel's sudden appearance at the table brought a welcome sense of relief.

"Am I interrupting something?" he inquired, darting a curious glance from one to the other.

"No, not at all," Rayna said brightly, pulling out a chair. "Please join us."

He hesitated for a fraction of a second before taking a seat. "Miguel Castillo," he said with a cordial smile, extending his hand.

"Tyler Brockwell," he responded, clasping the man's hand firmly, wondering who he was and what part he played in Rayna's life.

"Tyler...Brockwell?" Miguel repeated, emphasizing his last name while sliding a quizzical look in Rayna's direction.

"Yes."

To fill the uncomfortable silence, she blurted out, "Miguel and I share the same office." No sooner had she uttered the words than she regretted them. She could happily kick herself for volunteering the information. She owed Tyler no explanation for anything or about anyone in her life. Why should she give a damn what he thought?

"If you don't mind, I'd like to call you later to conclude this...discussion," Tyler told her, his tone gentle yet decisive. "Or, you can call me. I'm staying at the Marriott."

She shook her head. "Sorry, no time. I'll be tied up in court all week."

He fixed her with an intense look. "I'd appreciate it if you could make some time." He rose, nodded to Miguel and strode away.

Feeling ill at ease, Rayna fell silent and fiddled with her napkin, knowing full well Miguel was patiently awaiting an explanation.

"Okay, *Chica*," he said at length. "Let's have it."

"Have what?"

He looked at her squarely. "I'm assuming that guy you were talking to, who by the way, looks like he stepped off the cover of *GQ*, is some relation to Scott Brockwell?"

"His father."

"Oh? And you were talking to him why?"

"We weren't discussing the case. It just so happens that we're from the same town back in South Carolina. It's no big deal." She gave him a careless shrug.

He cocked his head sideways and fixed her with an expectant look. "Hey, it's Miguel you're talking to, remember? I could have recharged my car battery with the electricity generated between the two of you."

"Quit exaggerating. You're reading way too much into this."

"Am I? I think maybe you're fooling Rayna, but you sure as hell aren't fooling me."

Was she that easy to read? Had Tyler seen through her too? "Maybe I should impress upon you that I'm not in the habit of getting involved with married men." Anxious to escape his scrutiny, she darted a glance at her watch and exclaimed, "You know what? I don't have time for lunch. Gotta be in court in fifteen minutes." She picked up her purse and the folders. "But, I'll take a rain check."

"Not so fast."

"What?" She cringed inwardly, hoping he would not press her for more answers. She needed some time alone to digest everything that had happened.

"Just a reminder about tonight. We'll see you at around six, okay?"

Rayna stared at him blankly. "Tonight? What's happening tonight?"

His shoulders sagged. "Did you forget? Hello? It's Ricky's birthday party. Angelina is making her special enchilada casserole just for you."

Rayna fumbled in her purse, pulled out her day planner and flipped through the pages. "Oh, my God, that's tonight? I must have forgotten to write it down."

He frowned his disappointment. "So, you're not coming?"

She hesitated. "Of course I am, but I'll probably be late because I haven't even bought him a gift. I'll stop at the mall on my way."

"Don't sweat it."

"Right, like I'm going to disappoint your little boy by showing up empty-handed." She didn't have a clue as to what to buy the child and then a thought struck her. "Wait, I've got a better idea. Why don't you and Angelina bring the kids over to the zoo on Saturday? My treat. I'll be there all afternoon and I'll make sure you get in to see the baby tiger."

A wide grin spread across Miguel's face. "Sounds like fun to me! Catch you later."

Rayna blew him a kiss and headed back to her office. It was just as well she'd be around other people tonight. Playing with Miguel's three rambunctious children would keep her occupied and she wouldn't have as much time to think about Tyler and how deeply his unexpected appearance had affected her.

CHAPTER THREE

Tyler organized the paperwork he needed to fax to his office in the morning and then pushed to his feet, feeling restless once again. He roamed around the spacious living room of the two-bedroom hotel suite he shared with Scott. Thank heavens for Warren, he thought, heaving a grateful sigh. His brother-in-law's decision to join the family electronics firm last year had proved to be providential, especially now that he was committed to staying in Tucson for at least a few more weeks.

Remembering the grave expression on Freestone's face after the judge's declaration, he shuddered to think of what was in store for his son. Scott's behavior immediately following the accident seemed so coldhearted, so surprisingly out of character. And the victims—his heart twisted with pain every time he allowed himself to dwell on the extent of their injuries and the consequences awaiting Scott if one or both of them didn't survive their injuries.

He dropped onto the couch and closed his eyes, momentarily giving in to the gloom that rolled over him—the culmination of an incredibly long, debilitating day. He recognized the oncoming signs—icy dread settling like an anvil in his stomach and the beginning of what promised to be a massive headache. They were both symptoms of the oppressive moods he'd suffered for so many years and had only been free of these last eight months since his separation from Camille. It would have been easy to condemn her for this latest disaster, but he was by no means blameless. As a result of his own discontent, he'd

31

unintentionally meted out unhappiness to those around him. Okay, enough of that. He could do nothing to change the past. In a deliberate effort to banish the uncomfortable memories, he switched on the TV, hoping the incessant babble of the news anchors would distract him from Scott's horrific predicament and his inability to alter the lengthy and expensive legal minefield that lay ahead. What a hell of a mess.

Hands in his pockets, he rose and paced in aimless circles, finally stopping to admire the series of photographs decorating one wall. For the first time since his arrival ten days ago, he took the time to really study how the photographer had captured the startling beauty of Arizona. Each photograph depicted a different desert scene featuring windblown sand dunes and jagged crimson cliffs set against a sapphire sky filled with towering thunderheads. As a lifelong amateur photographer, he'd been itching to get outside of the city and put his new Nikon camera to good use.

The sudden ring of the telephone jolted him from his thoughts. Had Rayna changed her mind? He grabbed the receiver and eagerly pressed it to his ear. "Hello?"

"Scott?" a tentative female voice inquired.

"No, this is his father," he said, straining to hide his disappointment. "Who is this?" He was met with silence, a click and the dial tone. Annoyed, he dropped the phone onto the cradle. This was the third time in several days someone had hung up on him. He wondered if it was the same person. Too bad there was no caller ID on the hotel phone.

He looked up at the sound of the door opening. Scott sauntered in wearing baggy jeans and a ragged denim jacket. His shoulder-length blond hair looked stringy and in need of a good washing. It was an effort for Tyler to curtail the critical comments that leaped to his throat. Instead, he smiled in welcome. "Hi, I'm glad you're here early today. Maybe we can finally have dinner together."

Scott cast him a sullen look. "Can't. I'm going out with some guys from work tonight."

Accustomed by now to Scott's continual attempts to shun him, Tyler suppressed his displeasure. "Come on. I've been in town for more than a week and it seems the only time I ever see you is when we're meeting with Sheldon. Don't you think you and I should make an effort to have some alone time?"

"You forget I have a job," Scott mumbled, slumping into a chair and kicking off his sneakers.

Tyler felt his patience fading. "And that's another thing. I fail to see the point under the circumstances. You certainly don't need to be waiting tables now that I'm around."

There was a hard glint in Scott's pale blue eyes. "You always ragged on me about being responsible. I thought you'd be happy I was working."

"If you'd been trying to please me, you'd have stayed in school instead of taking off without a word and ending up here in the middle of this...this unbelievable mess."

Scott glowered at him. "My life was already a mess. You and Mom saw to that."

Tyler tightened his jaw. "I'm sorry as hell it finally came down to divorce, but the situation was intolerable for everyone concerned, especially you."

"Cool. I feel a lot better knowing your decision to split with Mom was made with my best interests at heart."

He picked up his shoes and marched into his bedroom, slamming the door behind him.

Tyler sighed in dismay. The one good thing, the *only* good thing that had come out of his volatile marriage to Camille was Scott. He remembered the first time he'd held him in his arms, how awestruck he'd felt, how full his heart had been. And even though he'd made a valiant effort, long hours at the plant combined with frequent out of town trips had made it difficult for him to establish a close relationship with Scott. There were so many things he should have done differently. Even with this latest tragedy, his efforts to help had apparently done little to diminish Scott's hostile attitude towards him. Tyler wondered how he was ever going to bridge the chasm separating them.

When Scott reappeared and headed wordlessly towards the door, Tyler called out to him. "Can we call a truce and plan dinner for tomorrow night?"

Scott paused, his hand on the doorknob. "I'm busy."

"Friday?"

"I'll have to see. Maybe," he said, pulling the door open.

"You let me know. By the way, someone's been calling for you."

Scott stopped abruptly and swung back, frowning. "Who?"

Tyler shrugged. "Damned if I know. Some woman. She hangs up as soon as she realizes I'm not you." For a split second, he thought he detected a trace of alarm in Scott's eyes. "Listen, if you've got a girlfriend...."

"I don't have a girlfriend," he cut in brusquely, shutting the door behind him.

Tyler studied the closed door pensively. Scott's evasive behavior was mystifying, to say the least. Clearly, he did know who was calling. Was his denial yet another attempt to shut him out of his life?

The sudden patter of rain on the window caught his attention. He switched the lamp off and stared at the rivulets of water streaming down the windowpane, blurring the city lights below. He fought the bleak shadow of loneliness settling over him and suddenly a spark of hope warmed him. Rayna was out there somewhere, no longer lost to him, the girl who had haunted his dreams all these years.

He still couldn't quite believe the strange and cruel circumstances that had brought her back into his life, a life that would have been so different had he followed his heart instead of bending to his father's iron will, to the devious coercion that had ruined so many lives.

Yes, she was back in his life, he thought, a bitter smile tightening his lips. Back to drive a spear through his heart, back to condemn him to desolation once again, this time by sending his only son to prison. He leaned his forehead against the cold glass. He'd never forgotten her. Never forgotten the sweet, lazy afternoons they'd spent together, her hand in his as they walked along the river, or her impish posturing every time he trained his camera lens on her. Most of all, he could never forget that last magical night.

He'd stolen away after his elaborate twentieth birthday party at the country club and met her at their secluded hideaway in the cove of trees down by the river's edge. The pale dusk had ushered in a giant, amber Carolina moon that crowned the distant mountains and filtered through the boughs of the fir trees where they lay entwined in each other's arms. They'd shared their dreams and repeated vows of love, their bliss marred only by the heavy burden he carried that night. It had taken every ounce of courage he had to tell her they could not see each other again until he persuaded his family to overlook her humble social status and accept her for what she meant to him. When she'd reluctantly agreed to a temporary separation, he had kissed away her anguished tears and given his solemn promise that some day soon they would be together forever.

***

Early Friday evening, struggling with an umbrella, case files and an armload of dry cleaning she'd been meaning to pick up for three weeks, Rayna unlocked the door of her condo and toed it open. She laid everything on the breakfast bar, then pulled off her soggy shoes, wishing she'd paid more attention to the weather forecast and worn her boots. The Pacific storm that had blown in Wednesday night had already dumped a record three inches of rain. And for a state that received only seven inches of rain annually, it was blessing but at the same time, had created big problems with flooding. The parking lot now resembled a small lake.

She looked out the balcony door and watched the fronds of the nearby palm trees whip back and forth in the brisk wind. To the east, dark clouds swirled around the summit of the Catalina Mountains. She couldn't decide if it was the unusually gloomy weather that had her in such a blue funk, or her preoccupation with Tyler—a predicament she never expected to confront in Tucson, after so many years, and under such inconceivable circumstances.

She hadn't been herself since their bizarre meeting on Wednesday. Even Miguel had commented on her distracted frame of mind later that same evening. He'd mentioned it again this morning. "What's the deal?" he'd demanded, waving a handful of messages from Tyler. "Why aren't you returning these calls? Come on, the Rayna I know never met a problem she couldn't handle."

"Miguel, leave it alone."

"Look, I don't know what happened between you and this Brockwell guy, and I sure as hell don't want to pry into your personal life, but sooner or later you're going to have to face the music. You can't hide from him forever."

"I'm not hiding," she shot back.

"Then why not call him?"

"I don't want to talk about it." His sudden silence and wounded expression caused instant remorse. "I'm sorry. It's rather complicated."

"No shit. Along comes your big chance to make up for the Stratton fiasco and you've got a real ethical dilemma going on. Not good. Not good at all."

Miguel couldn't have been more on target, Rayna thought, as she carried the dry cleaning to her bedroom and stripped off her damp blouse, replacing it with a warm turtleneck before returning to the kitchen. Even if she did manage to evade Tyler until the trial, how could she, in good conscience, proceed? Did she really believe that she could handle the case in an impartial, professional manner, that her past relationship with him would have no bearing on her ability to do her job? She had loved him more than any other human being on the face of the earth. If she only dared to admit it, the truth was that Tyler's unexpected intrusion into her well-ordered life had sent her senses spinning out of control, jeopardizing her disciplined existence.

Not only had she not been herself from the moment she'd seen him in the courtroom, she hadn't had a decent night's sleep since. Miguel certainly hadn't had any trouble identifying her perplexing situation. Even Tracy had told her she seemed uncharacteristically edgy last night at the gym.

Beauregarde's plaintive yowl startled her. "Well, hello, sweetie," she said softly, kneeling to scratch him under the chin. "You need a little attention, don't you?"

In obvious agreement, he threw himself down at her feet and rolled onto his back. She caressed his tummy, jumping slightly at the jangle of the phone. "Know what?" she said, staring into his hypnotic blue eyes, "One of these days I'll teach you to answer that thing."

She reached for the phone, but jerked her hand away, not recognizing the number displayed. What if it was Tyler? What would she say to him? Her throat dry as sawdust, she stood motionless, waiting for the message to begin. As Gary Sykes's voice filled the room, she convinced herself the weakness invading her bones was pure relief. So why did she feel totally deflated? She grabbed the cordless phone. "Hi, Gary."

"Oh, hey there. I was just about to leave you another message. Seems like you're never home."

"I just walked in. It's been an eventful week."

"I know exactly how you feel," he said, in an overly cheerful voice. "I've had a couple of super busy days myself lately, so I'm more than ready for a nice evening at the theater with good company tomorrow."

"I'm looking forward to it too," Rayna filled in automatically.

"By the way, you were right about the Green Lantern. They're closed for remodeling. How does Italian food sound instead?'

"Fine. Where?" She wondered if he detected the impatience in her voice.

"Have you ever been to Giovanni's?"

"I don't think so."

"If that sounds good to you, I'll pick you up at six."

"I'll be ready." She set the phone down, feeling detached and more than a little disturbed to realize that she was actually disappointed that it hadn't been Tyler. What made her think it might be him? Her number was unlisted.

She scooped the cat into her arms and buried her face in his soft fur. "Oh, Beauregarde, what am I going to do? Damn him for barging into my life again."

She'd no sooner spooned out the cat's dinner than the phone rang again. This time it was Tracy. "I called the office and they said you left early. Are you feeling all right?"

"Just tired. I brought a ton of work home for the weekend."

"Speaking of that," Tracy continued, "I wanted to make sure you'll be at the zoo by noon tomorrow. I've got to run to the airport to pick up Kevin's cousin from Chicago, so I might be a little late."

"No problem. I planned to be early anyway because I invited Miguel to bring his kids."

"By the way, he's single."

"Who's single?"

"Frank, Kevin's cousin."

Rayna rolled her eyes at Tracy's relentless crusade to find her a husband, and was about to counter with a biting remark when she heard a knock. "Hang on a second, that's probably Mrs. Ansel coming for her daily update on my activities." She moved to the door, pulled it open and froze in astonishment at the sight of Tyler Brockwell standing in the hallway.

CHAPTER FOUR

"Tracy," Rayna said, her heart beating so loudly she feared he would hear it, "I'm going to have to call you back." She clicked the off button, still staring at Tyler in disbelief. "How...how in the world did you find me? Who told you where I live?"

"No one," he whispered vaguely, so overcome by her appearance, he could barely speak. She looked amazingly young, standing there shoeless, the red turtleneck sweater accentuating her full breasts, a cloud of dark hair framing her oval face. She was such a disarming vision he almost had to pinch himself. This was no illusion, no part of the fantasy he'd clung to for so long, but the real flesh and blood woman. "I followed you."

"What?"

Noting the flare of agitation in her eyes, he assumed an air of innocence. "I apologize for intruding, but since you refused to return my calls, I had no choice."

"We all have choices."

Her remark wasn't lost on him. "Rayna, please. I just need a few minutes. I'm totally harmless. Scout's honor."

It was the first time she'd seen him smile and the years seemed to melt away. All of a sudden, she viewed him with new eyes. Indeed, there was nothing threatening about this tall, docile-mannered man standing before her, his handsome face touched with rain. It was an effort not to respond in kind. Be careful, she warned herself. It was important—no, critical—that she not let her guard down.

41

She eyed his damp jacket. "Apparently you forgot to bring a raincoat."

"I was told it never rains here," he said, keeping his voice light, gratified to see a look of acceptance replace the tension on her face. He'd carefully rehearsed what he would say as he'd kept a safe distance behind her black Acura. But now that he was in her presence and standing on her threshold, maintaining a calm façade seemed as difficult as balancing on the head of a pin. "So...do you want to talk here or may I come in?"

After hesitating a few more seconds, Rayna moved aside to let him pass, hoping she'd made the right decision. She closed the door and turned to stand with her back against it. "I can't discuss the case."

"I understand." He did his best to sound agreeable. He was determined not to antagonize her this time. "May I?" he asked politely, unbuttoning his jacket.

She nodded, took the jacket and hung it on the coat rack, while still questioning the wisdom of inviting him in. When she turned to face him again, she pressed her palms together tightly. "I'm not sure it will do either of us any good to talk about Summersville."

"Fair enough."

His intense look seemed to be at odds with his assenting tone. She stiffened, responding to the tension now suspended between them—a tension laden with suppressed accusations and unresolved questions. A sudden crash of thunder sliced the heavy silence and sent Beauregarde skittering to her side. The cat let out a mournful wail and pressed himself against her legs. "It's okay, baby," she assured him in a calm voice, bending to stroke his back.

All at once, his fear apparently forgotten, Beauregarde ambled away from her, strolled towards Tyler and flopped at his feet. "And who might this friendly creature be?" he asked with a grin, kneeling to allow the cat to sniff his hand.

"His name is Beauregarde."

"A fine Southern name," he murmured, rubbing the cat's fur briskly.

Rayna self-consciously crossed to the end table and switched on her favorite glass-domed antique lamp, which flooded the living room with amber light. "Please come in and sit down," she said formally, clearing her throat to stabilize the tremor in her voice.

Tyler settled on the couch and Beauregarde jumped into his lap. "Cats like me," he stated with a disarming grin as he scratched behind the cat's ears.

"So I see." Perched on the edge of the high-backed chair opposite him, she refrained from mentioning that Beauregarde was usually wary of strangers. She was both surprised and somewhat perplexed that he'd taken to Tyler with such ease.

Tyler studied her, his gaze lingering on her shapely legs as she attempted to tug the slim gray skirt lower on her thighs. She looked every bit as desirable in her stylish clothes as she did when she was a small-town girl clad in a simple cotton blouse and cut-off blue jeans.

"I like the way you've decorated this place," he said, shifting his attention to the furnishings that, while conservative, conveyed an artistic flair. And yet, he mused, surveying the tall arrangement of willowy dried flowers on the glass-topped coffee table between them, there were familiar vestiges of the past. She had always loved flowers, and there were flowers everywhere—in the antique milk can near the front door, in a vase that sat on the breakfast bar, and in baskets scattered throughout the living room.

43

Crisp scenes flashed through his mind as he recalled the first bouquet he'd picked for her. She'd lovingly pressed each blossom into the book of poetry he'd given her on their third date. He scanned the ceiling-high bookcase behind her, in the faint hope of seeing the familiar red and gold binding. He didn't. "So, how long have you been collecting antiques?" He hated the mindless chitchat, but what choice did he have? She'd set the rules for discussion.

"A friend of mine got me interested about five or six years ago. There's a lot to learn."

He was tempted to ask if the friend was male or female.

Rayna read the question in his eyes. Funny, she thought, that's how it used to be. They could reach into each other's minds, finish each other's sentences, like soul mates who'd spent a lifetime together rather than a couple of teenagers who'd only known each other for a few months. An unconscious sigh escaped her. Those halcyon days of long ago had brimmed with passion and love. They were innocent happy times. The happiest.

"Listen," Tyler said before the thunder-punctuated silence could close in on them. "I'd like to apologize for coming on so strong the other day."

"I think we were both taken off guard by the moment," she answered, sitting up stiffly.

He noted with dismay the wariness that had returned to her eyes, as if she were viewing a complete stranger. There was a gnawing in his gut, almost a physical pain, when it suddenly dawned on him how little he knew about this woman. The shy girl of yesterday now seemed uncannily different as she sat before him poised, assured, and breathtakingly beautiful. "So...how is your family?" he asked. "I lost track of them after your father died."

"That was fifteen years ago."

"What happened to your little brother? He had cerebral palsy, didn't he?"

"Yes."

He pressed on in spite of her shuttered expression. "How is he?"

"My mother took Adam to Vermont to live with my aunt. He got great medical care, but...he's been gone almost ten years."

"I'm truly sorry to hear that. And your mother?"

"She passed away two years ago."

Nodding somberly, he said, "My parents are both gone now too."

"It's never easy." Rayna grew wary. He was venturing ever so slowly into forbidden territory, but since he had, she had a few questions of her own. Perhaps it was time to plunge into the quicksand of the past. "Tell me, Tyler, how is Camille?"

Her direct question caught him by surprise. So, the gloves were off. "At this moment, I don't have the slightest idea," he replied, his tone hard, detached.

She arched a brow. "You don't have the slightest idea? One of those modern enlightened marriages I take it?"

He fixed her with a piercing gaze. "Hardly. We've been separated for almost a year now."

Rayna swallowed her astonishment, bewildered by the sudden, unreasonable rush of exhilaration. "How unfortunate." She hoped he wouldn't notice the breathlessness in her voice.

"Not at all. And if it weren't for the fact that she and her attorneys are holding out on the property settlement, the divorce would have been final by now."

She studied him for a moment, feeling unsure about the tumultuous emotions his announcement triggered. Was it regret? Was it sorrow for wasted happiness? Or did she feel a shameful sense of vindictiveness? "So it was not the perfect storybook marriage that you expected?" She regretted letting the sarcasm steal through, but she couldn't stop herself.

The harsh note in her voice stunned him. Feeling as though his face were suddenly on fire, Tyler hunched forward ready to retaliate. "Since you brought up the subject, let's get the record straight, shall we? *I'm* not the one who got married first, *you* did."

Rayna sprang to her feet and moved to the balcony door, her mood now as black as the clouds racing across the oppressive sky. Her back to him, she seethed aloud, "My actions were based on the fact that your engagement announcement to social butterfly and beautiful debutante Camille Hillenbrand just happened to be in the Summersville Gazette the day after you asked me to be patient, the day after you promised me we'd be...."

"My mother placed the announcement without my knowledge," he interjected. "I wanted to explain all that to you, but you were so damned stubborn I never got the chance! How did you think I felt when I heard you'd skated out of town and married someone else within a week's time? And that's another thing," he said, his voice rising. "Just how long did you have that guy waiting in the wings?"

She spun around to face him, her eyes blazing. "Unlike you, I had no one waiting in the wings. Thomas had been a family friend ever since I could remember, but that has nothing to do with the issue."

Tyler set Beauregarde on the couch and rose to his feet, jamming his hands into his pockets. "It has *everything* to do with it. I wanted to call the engagement off."

"Oh really? But you went ahead and married Camille anyway."

His jaw tightened. "There was a lot more at stake than you might think. And besides," he said, leveling a steely gaze at her, "what did you expect me to do? Sit around and lick my wounds the rest of my life?"

His wounds? For an instant Rayna saw red. His sanctimonious, self-centered attitude infuriated her. At least he'd had a wife, a family—all the things she knew she'd unconsciously denied herself because she'd been stupid enough to mourn the loss of this man's love.

They stood staring at each other, their eyes locked in mutual accusation until a sudden rap on the front door forced a truce between them. Rayna drew in a long, calming breath. She welcomed the reprieve the unforeseen interruption offered, even though she was certain the fireworks would resume later. Throwing him a reproachful look, she marched to the door and swung it open.

"Hello, dear," Mrs. Ansel said cheerfully. "My, what a storm! They're saying on TV that traffic's tied up something awful. The streets are flooded, cars stuck in washes, it's a real mess."

"I'm kind of in the middle of..." Rayna began, feeling slightly off balance at the unexpected visit.

"It's a good thing you're home early today safe and sound," the woman continued as if she hadn't spoken. "And please don't be mad at me now for tempting your sweet tooth again, but I baked a peach pie this afternoon

47

and I brought you a big slice. It's still nice and warm." Mrs. Ansel's free hand suddenly flew to the jumbled rows of pink curlers on her head when she spotted Tyler in the living room. She looked sharply at Rayna. "My goodness, why didn't you tell me you had a friend here? I hope I'm not intruding."

"Oh no, Mrs. Ansel, not at all." She hesitated, wondering whether to grab the pie and send her neighbor away, or use her fortuitous appearance to postpone the hostile discussion a little longer. She mustered a tight smile and gestured in his direction. "This is Tyler Brockwell. He's from my home town back in South Carolina."

Tyler let the tension slowly ebb from his body as he directed a polite bow towards the elderly woman. "Most pleased to make your acquaintance, Ma'am."

Mrs. Ansel's blue eyes sparkled with interest. Her pale complexion took on a pink hue as she laid a hand limply against her flat bosom. "Ohhh! I *love* your accent! You remind me of my Eldon. He was such a gentleman too."

"You're very kind," he said, making full use of the interruption to allow his temper to cool down and his heart rate to decrease.

Rayna gratefully accepted the pie. "Would you like to come in for a few minutes?"

"Oh, no, I couldn't. I look a sight," she fussed, fidgeting with the top button of her housecoat, but clearly pleased by the invitation.

"You look perfectly fine to me," Tyler said with a gracious smile.

Rayna slanted him a look to let him know that he was taking undue liberties and to remind him he was on tenuous ground before she strode into the kitchen. She snapped off a piece of aluminum foil to cover the pie, while half-listening to their conversation, which quickly progressed to friendly banter. It was obvious that Mrs. Ansel had succumbed to Tyler's charm.

Rayna shook her head wryly, unable to suppress a certain degree of admiration for the man's unabashed tenacity. She returned to the living room just as Mrs. Ansel was remarking that her late husband had always told her she resembled Maureen O'Hara, a well-known actress from the 1940s.

"Oh yes, I can certainly see the resemblance," Tyler agreed in a serious tone.

The look on her neighbor's face, blue eyes misting with gratitude, conveyed to Rayna that underneath his flattering responses lay genuine kindness. But she'd already known that. She remembered how he'd always taken the time to speak to her mother and spend a few moments with her brother, treating him as an equal and not as a helpless child in a wheelchair.

Mrs. Ansel edged forward. "So, Mr. Brockwell...."

"Please call me Tyler."

She gave him an appreciative nod. "Tyler, are you here on business?"

He darted Rayna a guarded look. "Not entirely."

"Your first visit?" she pressed.

"Yes, as a matter of fact it is."

"I'm sorry about the awful weather."

Tyler grinned. "I'm certain if you could do anything about it, you would."

She flushed. "I surely would. This is usually our nicest time of year. I hope Rayna will take the time to show you some of Arizona's outstanding landmarks," Mrs. Ansel rattled on. "The Grand Canyon is an absolute must, and then there is Monument Valley and..." she paused, as if suddenly aware she'd intruded on them, and blushed with embarrassment. "Listen to me chattering on. I'm probably interfering with your dinner plans. Oh, which reminds me, I only brought one piece of pie. Let me run and get another," she said, rising to her feet.

Rayna put up a hand. "No, that won't be necessary."

"But I want to. I can't possibly eat the entire pie all by myself."

"No, please don't," Rayna insisted, not wishing to prolong her visit and, consequently, Tyler's. "One slice is plenty."

"Well, all right, I'll be going then. It was *so* nice to meet you."

Tyler moved closer to Rayna. "Mrs. Ansel, the pleasure was all mine."

Glowing with delight, the older woman stepped into the hallway, but suddenly turned back to Rayna, with a speculative gleam in her eyes. "By the way, if you two do go sightseeing, be sure you take him to Madera Canyon. It's lovely there at sunset. And don't forget the Kartchner Caverns. They're nothing short of amazing. Also, there's Tombstone and Bisbee and...oh my, there are so many interesting places, I can't even think of them all."

"We'll probably get rained out this weekend," Rayna said, uncomfortably aware that Tyler stood only inches from her.

"Oh, let's hope not," Mrs. Ansel said, a sympathetic frown crinkling her forehead. "That would ruin things for you at the zoo tomorrow."

Rayna was losing patience. Given the chance, Mrs. Ansel would volunteer all of her personal business. "Thank you again for the pie."

"You kids have fun." She shuffled away and Rayna closed the door. At the click of the latch, she felt an uneasy hush engulf the room. Not in the mood for another stressful confrontation, she turned to face Tyler. "Let's not talk about Summersville anymore. There's nothing to be gained by dredging up old wounds and laying blame."

"I suppose you're right," he agreed reluctantly. He desperately needed to talk and clear the air, but didn't want to press her. "But I still hope somewhere down the road we can wipe the slate clean."

"I don't think so. What happened between us was a long time ago in another life. Those two people don't exist anymore."

"Perhaps not," he said, his eyes never leaving her face. "But *we* exist. What do you say we start over?" In response to her puzzled expression, he stretched to his full height and pressed a hand to his chest with a theatrical flair.

"Ma'am, allow me to introduce myself," he said, inclining his head. "My name is Tyler Carson Brockwell. I'm thirty-eight years old and I'm from Summersville, South Carolina. I own and operate Brockwell Industries, an electronics firm I inherited from my father. I would have preferred to pursue a career in photography, but since I was the only male offspring...well, you know," he said with a dismissive shrug. "I'm also kind to animals and strangers. I don't smoke and drink only sparingly. Granted my sock drawer is usually a mess, but on the other hand I'm never grouchy in the morning and I don't snore. Most important of all, I make the best barbeque sauce east of the Mississippi." His eyes twinkled with mischief.

"Your resume is most impressive, Mr. Brockwell," she said, cautiously playing along, "but aren't you oversimplifying things just a bit? And do keep in mind I'm not as susceptible to your southern charm as Mrs. Ansel is."

He could tell that she was trying to keep from smiling. "Okay," he said, folding his arms, "your turn."

"I never talk about myself on an empty stomach." Oops! She knew she'd made a mistake even as she'd said it.

"Okay," he said with boyish eagerness. "We'll continue after dinner."

"*We* are not having dinner," she said firmly. "I have a lot of work to do."

They both flinched when an ear-splitting crack of thunder shook the room. The lights blinked and Beauregarde streaked from the room as rain pounded against the sliding balcony door. Tyler tilted his head to one side, assuming a hangdog expression. "So, I'm to be banished out into the storm hungry?"

He looked so guileless she felt her resolve crumbling. "I'm afraid there isn't much to eat here. I was planning to have a bowl of cereal for dinner."

Arching one dark brow, he inquired, "Cereal? That's not a real dinner."

"I don't cook much. I don't have time."

"Hmmm. Well, I've been on my own for a while now and I've found cooking to be very therapeutic. If you have a few basic staples and some spices, I promise you'll be impressed with my culinary expertise."

Rayna wrestled with contradictory emotions. Now what? The safest and most prudent response would be to show him the door. The danger signals were all there, yet she foolishly chose to ignore them. "All right, you're on."

"Okay. Now then," he said, grinning broadly as he motioned towards the kitchen, "if you'll be so kind as to give me a brief tour of your pantry, I'll get things started."

As she led the way into the narrow kitchen, his close proximity made her skin feverish and her stomach quake, not unlike her reaction when facing the bar exam. It was the same fear of taking on a task too immense, too daunting, when she felt unprepared.

She opened one of the cupboards and the door to the small pantry. "Ah, polenta!" he exclaimed, setting the bag on the counter. "Good start." He rummaged around in the small pantry and emerged with cans of tuna, tomato sauce and mushroom soup. "Do you have basil and garlic?" he inquired, his eyes bright with expectation.

"Sure." She pointed to the spice rack, then pulled out the cookware. "I'll make a salad," she offered, trying to sound casual as she watched him confidently assemble the ingredients for dinner.

They worked together in silence as though abiding by an unspoken agreement and politely drew back each time they accidentally touched. Every innocent brush against him electrified her, shattering her concentration. All of a sudden, the simple task of throwing together a salad became a major production. Twice she opened the refrigerator and stood staring, unable to remember what she wanted. This was crazy. How could he possibly evoke such feelings in her after all these years, after all the pain he'd inflicted on her?

"Are you saving this for a special occasion?" he asked, pointing to the unopened bottle of chardonnay in the refrigerator.

"No." She reached for the corkscrew to open it.

"Here, let me do that," he said, his fingers briefly resting on hers before she quickly withdrew her hand and turned away, fearful he would notice the effect he was having on her.

An hour later, seated across from her at the breakfast bar, Tyler sipped the last of his wine and happily watched Rayna place her fork on the empty dinner plate with a satisfied sigh. "That was amazing. If I'd known this meal was going to be so exquisite," she remarked, unable to curb an appreciative smile, "I would have cleared off my dining room table that stubbornly insists on being a desk. I have to confess I underestimated your cooking skills."

Keeping his tone light, he drawled, "I hope to impress you with some of my other fine qualities. And by the way, the meal isn't over yet." He shot her an impish grin. "I do believe you are in possession of some freshly baked peach pie?"

Before she could respond he slid off the stool, peeled back the foil and set the plate halfway between them. Rayna had just finished congratulating herself. She'd managed to get through dinner as well as the unobtrusive conversation with flying colors, but the familiarity of sharing the same plate made her uneasy once again. She folded her hands together. "You know what? I'm stuffed. It's all yours."

Her body language signaled her discomfort, so he smiled and pulled the plate in front of him. "Mmmm," he sighed, after the first bite. "This is great." When she didn't respond, he asked, "I'm curious. What made you choose a career in law?"

She stiffened. What should be a simple answer wasn't. And it had only been after years of therapy that she'd come to the realization herself. How could she tell

him that the part he'd played in what proved to be the
pivotal event of her life, had been a major factor; that
because of it, she derived great personal satisfaction when
her efforts culminated in justice being served? "Let's just
say, it chose me," she responded evasively.

Her elusive tone warned Tyler that he was
encroaching on forbidden territory, so he switched gears,
remarking with enthusiasm, "I'll tell you what, I really like
Arizona." He took another bite of the pie and asked,
"So...how did you come to live here in Tucson?"

She shrugged. "Thomas's firm transferred him here.
I hated it at first. The heat, not having forests and
rivers...but now I love the mountains, the solitude of the
desert, the sunsets. I can't imagine ever leaving."

Tyler bit back the questions that burned in his mind.
Had she been happier in her marriage than he'd been in
his? Had she missed him as much as he had missed her?
More important, was there anyone special in her life now?
The thought sent a chill through him. Was he prepared for
her answer? His frustrated ruminations came to a halt
when he noticed her glance at her watch. "I guess I'd better
not overstay my welcome," he said softly, laying down his
fork. "Listen...if you have some spare time, I'd like to
follow up on your neighbor's suggestion. I don't suppose
you'd consider playing tour guide for me tomorrow?"

"I can't."

He hid his disappointment beneath a valiant smile.
"Oh, that's right, Mrs. Ansel said you do something at the
zoo on weekends? What do you do exactly?"

"I volunteer at the petting zoo on Saturday
afternoons. I enjoy being around the kids."

His expression brightened. "Well, that sounds like
an interesting photo opportunity. Mind if I come by?"

She tensed, torn between heeding the warning signals emanating from her logical mind and the purely emotional anticipation of seeing him again. "I really don't think that's a good idea."

"You won't even notice me," Tyler said with gentle insistence.

"It's a free country," she said with a resigned shrug.

Heartened, Tyler moved to retrieve his jacket from the coat rack. "Thank you for dinner."

"Thank *you* for cooking," she said, sliding off her stool to see him out.

He locked eyes with her. "I haven't enjoyed anything this much for...well, nineteen years."

Rayna swallowed hard. "Really?"

"Really."

After she closed the door behind him, she stood with her back against it, trying to decipher the myriad of emotions consuming her. She was in trouble. That much was certain. All evening, she'd rejected what her heart instinctively knew to be true. She still had feelings for this man. Considering the circumstances, considering the fact that she'd actually convinced herself that she hated him for what he had done, her intense attraction both disturbed and confounded her. The rush of bittersweet happiness could not allay the somber reality she faced. Aside from the baggage both she and Tyler carried from the past, which might or might not in time be resolved or forgiven, if she let her guard down, it would be impossible for her to continue prosecuting his son. Even if she elected to sacrifice her professional aspirations and withdraw from the case, her connection with the forces in motion that could send the boy to prison might constitute an insurmountable barrier between them.

No matter which way she looked at the situation, it came around to the same obvious conclusion. There could never be a happily-ever-after ending. This was a no-win situation. She must not see Tyler Brockwell again.

CHAPTER FIVE

Tyler's heart had lightened considerably by the time he parked his car at the hotel and ambled towards the entrance. The evening, having started out on shaky ground, had ended reasonably well. The apparent softening of Rayna's resistance was a good start to finding a favorable resolution to the animosity and resentment that obviously plagued each of them. Still he had his work cut out if he was to have any success breaking down the emotional barrier she had erected. Rayna's coldhearted rejection had haunted him his entire life, yet he'd been surprised and mystified by the depths of her animosity towards him during their heated exchange.

At least the rain had stopped. He inhaled deeply, finding the rain-washed wind invigorating. Overhead, a patchwork of starlit sky glimmered through the disintegrating storm clouds. Nice place, Arizona. The advent of good weather would allow him to see Rayna again tomorrow. It was providence, he decided, entering the elevator and punching the button with a jaunty stab of his finger. Perhaps his luck was changing after all. Perhaps his life was taking a turn for the better. Nevertheless, he cautioned himself not to read too much into the tenuous progress he'd achieved with her so far.

It had taken every ounce of willpower not to touch her. Man, you're in over your head now, he thought, noting his flushed reflection in the elevator's mirrored interior. But how in the world could he possibly cultivate a relationship with a woman who was bent on sending his son to prison? The thump of rap music surprised him as he approached his suite and inserted the plastic door card. Inside, Scott sat slouched on the sofa, absorbed in the wild gyrations of scantily clad women in a music video. "I didn't expect to find you here," he shouted, taking a seat beside his son.

"I've been waiting here for a couple of hours," Scott replied, his tone sullen.

Tyler eyed him, puzzled.

"Dinner. Remember? Just the two of us? I looked for you downstairs in the restaurant and coffee shop."

A pang of guilt shot through Tyler. "Oh. Right. Well...you never got back to me about it, so I made other plans. I'm sorry."

Scott shrugged and turned back to the TV. "Forget it, no big deal."

"Hey, we can go now. I've already eaten, but let's get you something."

"Never mind." Scott thumbed the remote, raising the sound level.

Tyler's emotions seesawed between twinges of regret and irritation. "Turn it off."

"What?"

"I said turn it off," he shouted, grabbing the remote.

"Okay," Scott replied, looking at Tyler with astonishment. "Chill out."

Tyler rose and paced, slowly counting to ten before facing his son. "I have put my life on hold for you and hired the best damned defense attorney money can buy. I don't expect a medal, but I do expect you to show me at least a modicum of respect. And a little appreciation might be nice too. You, son, are in one hell of a jam."

Scott chewed on a fingernail, then said, "I wouldn't have bothered you at all if I'd been able to get in touch with Mom, but she...."

"Well, you *didn't*," Tyler cut in impatiently. "The fact remains that *I'm* here and she's not."

"Sorry to put you out."

"Don't misinterpret what I'm saying," Tyler went on, straining to maintain his temper. "I'm well aware that I don't deserve the father-of-the-year award. There were far too many times when I wasn't there when you needed me."

"No shit," Scott retorted with unconcealed hostility.

Tyler let out a groan of frustration. "I know I failed you in a lot of ways, but I'm really not the villain your mother made me out to be."

"It didn't seem like you put yourself out a whole lot to make her happy either."

"You're going to have to cut me a little slack. I admit I made some mistakes, but I'm not going to take the blame for her drinking and misuse of prescription drugs. Sooner or later people have to accept responsibility for their own actions."

Scott stared at the floor.

"I'm sorry as hell things turned out the way they did," Tyler said, lowering his voice. "Your mother and I managed to bring out the worst in each other. Unfortunately you were caught in the middle."

"Yeah, well, life's a bitch."

Tyler closed his eyes momentarily, searching for the right words. "Listen, Scott, I know I was gone a lot, and the majority of times it was business-related, but sometimes...sometimes I just had to get away. Do you understand?"

"You mean like the time you cancelled the fishing trip you promised me and then got me the bike instead? What about the times you missed my birthday? Did you think that buying me an expensive guitar and all that other stuff would make up for it? And that car you bought me for graduation, did you think that made up for the fact that you weren't there?"

The pain reflected in his son's eyes saddened him. "I would never have intentionally missed your graduation. You know I couldn't do a damn thing about being stranded at the airport in Dallas. I can't alter what happened, but shutting me out of your life now isn't going to benefit either of us."

Scott's silence made Tyler feel as though he'd been talking to the couch. "Give it some thought," he said, anxious to open the lines of communication. "By the way, what *did* happen to the car I bought you?"

"It got messed up in a freeway pileup in Alabama," he mumbled.

"What? Why didn't you tell me? Were you hurt?"

"Naah, just a slight whiplash."

"Did you contact the insurance company?"

"I didn't feel like hanging around that little jerk-water town for them to settle, so I traded it for the SUV."

Tyler tried to conceal the outrage that had been building since he'd arrived in Tucson. "You traded a forty thousand dollar car for that junk heap?"

"It didn't look so new after getting mashed. Besides, you never even asked me if that's the kind of car I wanted."

He accepted the criticism and nodded slowly. "In hindsight, you're right. I should have asked you. But...I wanted it to be a surprise." Even though he was inwardly fuming, for the first time in a long while he felt hopeful. At least they were talking. "Come on, let's go downstairs and get you something to eat."

When the phone rang, Scott lunged to answer it. He pressed the receiver to his ear and stood in frozen silence.

"Who is it?" Tyler asked from the doorway, curious about Scott's surreptitious behavior.

"I can't talk now," Scott said in a barely audible whisper. "You promised you wouldn't...no! Stay there. I'll come and get you." He replaced the receiver and turned to meet his father's questioning look. "I...uh...have to give somebody a ride home."

"I'll go with you."

"No! I mean...it's okay. I'll be back later."

Tyler caught him by the shoulder as he rushed past him to the door. "Scott, is there something you're not telling me?"

He averted his eyes, muttering, "No, everything's cool."

Tyler gave his son's arm a reassuring squeeze. "In spite of everything that happened back home and here, I hope you know you can to talk to me about anything."

Scott gave him a thin smile. "Thanks, Dad."

After watching him bound out the door, Tyler returned to the sofa, burdened with concern. The phone calls from the unknown female, the puzzling behavior—there was little doubt that Scott was harboring a secret. If only there were something he could do or say to gain his trust.

Eyes closed, head resting against the cushions, his mind backtracked to the last few wondrous hours he'd spent with Rayna. He experienced an inner peace he had not felt for ages. Now, more than ever, he looked forward to seeing her again.

* * *

Amid the shouts and laughter of two dozen or so children roaming the grounds of the petting zoo, Rayna kneeled down to wrap a comforting arm around Miguel's three-year-old son, Ricky. "He won't hurt you, sweetie," she soothed as a black and white Angora goat approached him. "Suki loves little boys."

"Will he bite me?" the child asked warily.

"No. If you stand very still, he may even give you a kiss."

As if to prove her right, the goat, now eye-to-eye with Ricky, stretched closer, pushed out his snout and flicked his pink tongue along the boy's neck. Giggling, he said, "That feels tickly." He turned around to make sure his father was nearby. Sitting on one of the concrete benches scattered throughout the fenced-in area of the zoo, Miguel laughed and waved to his youngest son.

Wistfully, Rayna wondered again what it would have been like to have a child of her own. She brushed aside the momentary sadness and gave the boy an affectionate squeeze. She loved children. Volunteering a few hours a week gave her the chance to enjoy them as well as do a good turn for the community.

She waved to one of the other volunteers. "Carol, watch the kids for a minute, will you?"

"Okay."

"Let's go see your daddy," she said, swinging him into her arms. She wound through clusters of children, goats and sheep, finally depositing him on Miguel's lap.

"Why don't you take him in the red barn to see the rabbits and chickens? They're probably more his speed." Shading her eyes against the blinding sun, she peered through the tall stands of bamboo along the sandy path beyond the fence. "Where did your other two kids disappear to?"

Miguel aimed his thumb over his shoulder in the direction of the cages by the lagoon. "They're over there teasing the squirrel monkeys. Hey, thanks for getting us in to see the tiger cub. That was a super birthday gift. Thanks again."

"No problem. I'm glad you're all enjoying yourselves." Her eyes strayed again to the front gate and she suppressed a wave of disappointment. Apparently Tyler had decided not to come after all.

"Waiting for someone?" Miguel asked, lifting a questioning brow.

"Tracy. She's late." Even though that was a fact, she felt a mild jab of guilt for not telling Miguel the whole truth.

Ricky nudged his father impatiently. "Daddy, I want to see the wabbits!"

Miguel stood up. "Okay, big guy, let's go check 'em out."

Rayna convinced herself that it was actually a good thing Tyler hadn't come today. How on earth would she have explained it to Miguel? She fell into step beside him only to hear Tracy call out from behind, "Wait up!" Wheeling around, she smiled as her friend came rushing up. "There you are."

"Sorry. I didn't mean to be so late. The plane was delayed. Hey there, Miguel," Tracy added, buttoning her green smock. "Haven't seen you in a month of Sundays. Where's Angelina?"

"At home. Her feet are pretty swollen."

"She hasn't had it too easy with this pregnancy, has she? You should be ashamed of yourself," Tracy teased, slapping his arm lightly. "Why don't you leave her alone?"

"She's the one who wanted another kid," Miguel protested with a wicked smile. "I was just doing my job. And I think I did it pretty good." He disappeared inside, his contagious laughter echoing after him.

"It must be a blast working in the same office with him," Tracy said, grinning.

"It is."

"Wow, this place is packed today."

"You could say it's been a real zoo," Rayna quipped.

"Ha. Good one. I didn't think *that* many people would show after the storm. Look at the puddles! We'd better make sure the kids don't fall in."

"Two already have," Rayna remarked wryly, wiping traces of dried mud from her smock. "Listen, will you keep an eye on things while I get the brushes?"

"Sure." Three boys rushed past them in hot pursuit of a curly Pygmy goat. "You know how much I love the little monsters."

Rayna turned away, sneaking one final glance towards the park entrance before entering the supply room. Under her breath, she chastised herself. "He isn't coming. Quit acting like a lovesick teenager." She pulled baskets of plastic brushes from the shelf, all the while wrestling with the ridiculous urge to weep. What was wrong with her? There was no room in her life for such nonsense. Outside again, a few deep breaths of cool air soothed her jittery nerves. She put on a happy face and handed out the brushes to the children, with patient instructions on how to properly use them on the animals.

"Don't groom them too hard," Tracy instructed the excited children. "And be careful of their eyes."

Rayna suddenly sensed she was being watched. Looking up, her heart contracted when she spotted Tyler standing outside the low chain-link fence, camera in hand. She sprang to her feet, painfully aware of the awful picture she must present in faded jeans, her muddy smock bulging with candy wrappers and other paraphernalia she'd picked up around the yard. Her hands flew to smooth the stray hairs that had escaped from her ponytail.

Tyler couldn't resist snapping half a dozen shots. Surrounded by the goats and laughing children, Rayna looked as disarmingly fresh and natural as a field of sunflowers. It brought back heartwarming recollections of the first time he'd seen her—a young girl in an oversized plaid shirt and rolled-up blue jeans. Bare feet dangling in the water, she'd been fishing at the edge of a stream, her face raised to the wind, her long black hair fluttering behind her. She'd been with an older man he later learned was her father. Undetected, Tyler had snapped a series of pictures with a telephoto lens.

Never would he forget the shock of seeing her behind the counter at the photo shop a few days later when he picked up the prints. Nor could he forget the stunned expression on her face when she recognized herself in the pictures. The instant their eyes met, he knew his life would never be the same.

"Stud alert!" Tracy exclaimed under her breath as Tyler opened the gate. Rayna stood breathless watching him stride towards them. The black crew-neck sweater accentuated his broad shoulders and dark blue jeans emphasized his slim hips.

"Hello," he said, a slight smile teasing the corners of his mouth.

"Hi." She couldn't seem to think of anything else to say. For seconds, they stood staring at each other until Tracy cleared her throat with forced exaggeration. "Rayna usually introduces me to her friends, but apparently not today."

"Oh, I...I'm sorry," Rayna stammered, forcing her gaze away from his to meet Tracy's inquisitive one. "Tracy, this is Tyler Brockwell. I've known him for...I mean we...we're both from South Carolina. Originally," she added, feeling inane. What was the matter with her?

"Delighted to meet you," he said, accepting her outstretched hand, amusement dancing in his dark eyes. Grinning ear to ear, Tracy turned wide mischievous eyes on Rayna. "Well, I'm going to go now and leave you two alone. I'm sure you have a lot of catching up to do."

Rayna could have cheerfully smacked her friend for deserting her and struggled to regain her composure. "Ah...I didn't think you were coming."

"Why? I wouldn't have missed photographing you in this setting."

"I look terrible," she murmured, self-consciously, flicking wisps of straw from her jeans. Intelligent conversation seemed to have eluded her. "Turned out to be a perfect day weather-wise," was all she could finally articulate.

"It's more than that. It's a blue sky day," he said softly with a reminiscent smile. "Do you remember that?"

Remember? How could she ever forget the special phrase they'd lovingly exchanged during those six fairytale months? Something akin to resentment rose up inside her. How was it possible that this man could barge into her life after all this time and arouse emotions she'd thought were carefully in check? She refrained from commenting and strove to appear indifferent. "Oh, yes, I'd forgotten." Her heart sank at the sight of Miguel walking towards her, his three children in tow.

"Hi, Miguel, do you remember Tyler Brockwell?" It was an effort to sound blasé.

"Yes, I do," he said, returning Tyler's courteous nod.

"You're leaving already?" Rayna asked, tilting her head to one side.

"Yep, the little guy is tuckered out," he replied, squeezing the boy's shoulder. "We all had a great time. Thank you. See you later."

"Bye."

His backward glance left no doubt in her mind that she'd get an earful from him Monday morning.

"Do you have a few minutes to sit and talk?" Tyler asked, looking hopeful.

She hesitated. "I can't. I have to watch the kids."

"I'm sorry. I didn't mean to interfere. I'll just roam around and take a few more shots." He strolled towards the barn and Rayna turned to find Tracy staring a hole through her. "Okay, out with it. Where have you been hiding that luscious hunk?"

"I haven't been hiding him. He's just a…a guy I knew a long time ago."

"Really? Just a guy?"

"Yeah." She could tell by Tracy's skeptical frown that she wasn't buying her explanation.

"Why do I have a feeling there might be more to it than that? Okay, what's the story?"

"There *is* no story."

"Helloooooo! I may be a lot of things, but blind isn't one of them."

"Come on, Tracy. This isn't one of those romance novels you're always reading."

Tracy impatiently waved away her remark. "And I suppose this *guy*," she huffed, dragging out the word, "has nothing to do with your lukewarm behavior towards Gary and every other man I've fixed you up with."

"For your information, I'm seeing Gary tonight."

Loud laughter and the angry squeal of a child interrupted them. "Quick, look," she said, prodding Tracy to turn around. Across the yard, a toddler was waging a tug-of-war with a lamb latched onto the nipple of his bottle. As she rushed to aid the child's mother, Rayna couldn't help noticing Tyler kneeling nearby, snapping pictures of the mini-drama. She stuck her finger in the lamb's mouth, disengaging the nipple with a loud pop. In the midst of loud laughter from the throngs of children, the parents applauded as the toddler fell into his mother's arms and the lamb scampered away bleating in protest. With the excitement over, the crowd quickly dispersed and Rayna's pulse rate shot up as Tyler approached her. Damn he looked good. Unable to think of anything else to say, she admonished him with mock severity. "You could have given the kid a hand."

"And spoil a priceless shot like that? Not on your life. By the way, you're very photogenic. But, then...you always were."

His words affected her like a physical caress and her cheeks burned, remembering the afternoon she'd posed for him in the nude. She'd been amazed when he'd shown her the pictures developed in his new dark room—neither lurid nor suggestive, but artistically done using a wonderful blend of light and shadow. At her insistence, he'd destroyed the negatives and handed over all of the pictures to her. She dared not take a chance that they would fall into the hands of her father. If he had any idea of how far their relationship had gone...she'd shuddered to think of his reaction.

"Janet's here now," Tracy announced with a playful lilt in her voice, "so if you two kids want to run along and play, we can handle it from here."

Rayna took advantage of her calculated remark. "Actually, that would be great. I brought home a ton of work and haven't even looked at it."

"Off with you then," she ordered, but then added with sly tone, "Hey, don't forget the auction tomorrow. We have to be there before two o'clock."

Rayna glowered at her friend. What was she doing?

"Auction?" Tyler inquired politely.

Tracy smiled brightly. "Yes. At my mother's antique shop. You're welcome to come if you're interested. It's kind of out in the boondocks, but it's well worth the trip if you're into that kind of thing."

Rayna winced inwardly. Being forced to see him again tomorrow would only heighten her distress, but she felt obligated to attend the auction since Tracy's mother had generously agreed to include her armoire in the sale. It was not the first time Mrs. Butler had helped unload some of her more impulsive purchases.

"Ever get any old camera equipment?" he asked, his face lighting with interest.

"Now and then."

"Well now, that sounds like a fun way to spend a Sunday afternoon." He shot a quick glance at Rayna to gauge her reaction, but she seemed to be making a point of looking anywhere but at him.

"Great." Tracy dug a crinkled card from her pocket and handed it to him. "Here's the address and there's a little map on the back." She turned to Rayna, her eyes sparkling. "I'll be at your place early so we can get that gargantuan armoire of yours loaded onto the truck."

"That sounds like a rather tall order for you two ladies to handle alone," Tyler remarked with a thoughtful look. "Do you need help?"

Tracy said, "Well, sure...."

"Thanks," Rayna cut in. "I've got it covered."

Tracy had obviously fallen for Tyler's charm as completely as had Mrs. Ansel. "I've got to go," she said tersely, unbuttoning her smock. "See you all later." She made it to the main gate before Tyler intercepted her.

"You're angry with me," he stated in a resigned tone, matching her stride. "I'm sorry if my coming here today upset you. And, if it's going to make you unhappy, I won't come to the auction tomorrow."

Rayna inhaled a calming breath. "I'm not upset. If you want to go tomorrow then by all means do so." She continued towards her car, stepping up her pace, all the while thinking how erratic and ludicrous her behavior must seem to others. How could anyone else understand? She'd been running from the past all of her adult life and now Tyler had finally chased her down. The question was, did she want to be caught? And if she dared let her guard down, was she prepared for the consequences?

"Have dinner with me tonight."

She stopped and met his steady gaze. "What?"

"Dinner. I'd like you to have dinner with me."

Rayna shook her head slowly, astounded at his persistence. "No, Tyler. I *can't*. Please don't make this situation more difficult than it already is."

"Why does it have to be difficult? We both have to eat."

"No!" She shook her head vehemently. "Don't you understand? We shouldn't even be talking to each other."

"What's the harm if it's not about the case?"

She opened the car door and slid behind the wheel. "I have a date tonight."

Tyler felt like he'd been kicked in the heart. "I see." He closed her door and stood back as she gunned the car out to the street. He watched her vanish from sight before slumping into the front seat of his rental car, where he grappled with monstrous feelings of frustration, hopelessness, and yes, jealousy.

He massaged the back of his neck. Who was she seeing? The thought of her in another man's arms, kissing another man's lips, sickened him. For a few fleeting seconds he entertained the irrational idea of spying on her tonight. Why did everything have to be so damned complicated? He couldn't deny that he was backing her into an ethical corner. Was he imagining it, or beneath her cool resistance did he sense her attraction to him?

The best solution for all concerned would be to walk away from her, suffer through the ordeal with Scott and then return to his former life. But his heart rejected the thought. He'd lost her once. This time he would do whatever it took to prevent that from happening again.

CHAPTER SIX

The rapid-fire monotone of the seasoned auctioneer announcing the pending sale of her armoire, prompted Rayna to turn away from the drop-leaf table she'd been inspecting and take an aisle seat in the third row of chairs facing the platform.

"Do I hear a thousand? Do I hear a thousand?" the tall, bony man barked into the microphone, his observant eyes searching the warehouse filled wall-to-wall with furniture and people. "Come on, folks. This is a fine piece," he prodded. "Do I hear seven-fifty?"

Rayna's heart shrank with disappointment as she cast a quick look around. So far, no one in the crowd had raised their numbered card to bid.

"Take a good look at it, people," the auctioneer cajoled. "Do I hear seven?" When the bid dropped to five hundred with no takers, Rayna glumly prepared for a big loss. She'd shelled out nine hundred originally and it had been crowding her spare room ever since, along with seven other pieces she hoped to get around to refinishing someday. Then, she perked up with renewed interest when the auctioneer shouted, "Thank you, sir! I've got five hundred. Do I have six? Do I have six? Thank you! Seven hundred? Yes! Do I have eight?"

Hardly believing her ears, Rayna listened with amazement as the bids steadily rose. It was difficult to restrain her excitement when the auctioneer bellowed, "Sold for twelve hundred dollars to number 14!" A three hundred dollar gain was not too shabby. She glanced

73

behind her, but could not tell who had bought the armoire. It was then she saw Tyler standing beside a table piled with tools and bric-a-brac. He seemed totally absorbed, closely examining an old Polaroid camera. They'd exchanged a brief, cordial greeting an hour ago. Surprisingly, he'd made no attempt to speak to her since, as though he were deliberately keeping his distance. She convinced herself she was not disappointed at all, but shifted restlessly in her seat, reviewing her rude behavior towards him yesterday. Cold embarrassment washed over her remembering how she'd peeled out in her car leaving him there in the dust. There was no excuse for such childish conduct and she certainly owed him an apology. But she was hesitant to approach him, fearful he would misinterpret her apology as a change of heart. Under the circumstances, perhaps keeping a safe distance was the wisest choice.

In hindsight, leaving the zoo early had been a waste of time. Her high emotional state made it impossible to concentrate on the work she'd brought home. And later, images of Tyler had persisted; intruding on what should have been a thoroughly enjoyable evening—dinner at Giovanni's and a well-acted, thought-provoking play. And Gary—attentive, witty and charming—would have most certainly qualified as the perfect date. But for all the pleasure it gave her, she may as well have been having lunch in the cafeteria with one of her colleagues.

"My feet are killing me," Tracy groaned, sliding into the adjacent chair. She slipped off her shoes and massaged her toes. "Congratulations! Looks like you made out like a bandit on that armoire."

Rayna gave her a wry smile. "I was lucky."

"So, now that you're rolling in cash, are you going to bid on that music box I know you're dying to have?"

"I'd love to, but I really can't justify buying a Reuge."

"Oh, come on. Mom said the movement is damaged, so it may not bid all that high. Hey, you might be able to pick it up for a song."

Rayna rolled her eyes. "You're hopeless."

Tracy laughed and surveyed the hall. "What a great turnout…well, well, look who's here. It's your mystery man."

"Would you quit it? He's not my mystery man."

"He is to me. Some best friend you are, not telling me about him."

"Tracy, there's nothing to tell."

"A little testy today, are we? Wait a minute. Did you cancel on Gary last night?"

"Of course not. Shhhh! There it is." Rayna edged forward in her chair, eyes riveted on the music box. It had been love at first sight when she'd spotted the rare find two hours ago nestled inside the glass display case. She'd circled it in silent reverence, her fingertips itching to touch the smooth hand-painted walnut grain, intricately inlaid with contrasting wood and brass. But beauty and workmanship aside, Rayna loved the uniquely pure sound that resonated from a Reuge. And in spite of the two hairline cracks and the card explaining that it skipped notes, it appeared to be in otherwise pristine condition.

Rayna's throat went dry. No doubt the bidding would be fierce. She'd noticed the other antique buffs covetously eyeing it. Wouldn't it be great if she could snap it up for the twelve hundred dollars she'd just gotten for her armoire? And who cared if it wasn't in perfect working order? Mrs. Butler would probably know someone who could repair it for a reasonable fee. *Dream on, Rayna.* Twelve hundred wouldn't even come close.

On the other hand, if she included the nine hundred and fifty dollars she had in savings, added the forty or so in her wallet...her adrenalin skyrocketed. All the good intentions to use today's proceeds to pay down her credit cards flew out the window as the auctioneer shouted the opening bid.

"I'll start at seven hundred." His slow wink indicated that he knew full well that the price would quickly escalate.

Rayna flashed her number.

"Thank you. Do I have eight hundred?" he asked, gesturing around the room. "Thank you, sir!" He looked back at Rayna. "Eight-fifty?" She nodded. "I see nine hundred," he said, pointing to the back of the room. "I need a thousand."

As the bidding exceeded Rayna's available cash, she cast aside common sense and allowed herself to be momentarily swept into the bidding rush. Her hopes were quickly dashed when the numbers crackled upward around her, forcing her to stop. As the auctioneer's gavel pounded on the final bid of thirty-four hundred, Rayna turned and begrudgingly nodded her congratulations to the ecstatic woman who was now the lucky owner of the music box.

Tyler stared at Rayna, mesmerized by her passionate involvement in the vigorous competition. Her fascination with the music box had been evident to him from the start. In fact, she'd appeared so entranced she hadn't even noticed his arrival or that he'd stood nearby waiting to greet her. It had been several minutes before she raised her eyes from the glass case.

And now, as he studied the expression on her flushed face change from rapt attention to dejection, his heart went out to her. He wished he'd outbid everyone else and acquired it for her. But it was probably just as well he hadn't. More than likely she would take offense at such an intimate gesture.

In the early hours of dawn, he'd decided it might be best to pull back for a while. Take things a little slower. But the frantic call from Warren a few hours later, warning of an imminent strike at the plant, changed everything. He'd managed to get a flight out that evening so he could meet with the union negotiators first thing Monday morning. The realization that he would not be able to see Rayna for several days depressed him greatly. Even though she'd made it perfectly clear that she could not associate with him, he had no intention of throwing in the towel. He drew in a deep breath and threaded his way through the crowd. As he grew near, she met his gaze head on. Was he mistaken, or had he caught a fleeting gleam of anticipation in her eyes? He straddled the chair directly in front of her and folded his arms on the back. "Too bad about the music box," he said with a sympathetic smile. "It's quite exceptional."

Rayna sat tongue-tied. She desperately wanted to convey indifference towards him, but could barely contain her delight. "Oh, it's...not that important," she finally managed to say. "Guess I can live without it. I have so far."

Tyler stiffened. Was there a subtle message in her words? A strained silence fell between them and continued so long that Tracy finally broke it. "Tyler, I'm really glad you decided to come. Are you going to bid on anything?"

"Possibly. I have my eye on a 1910 Leica camera and perhaps that original Polaroid over there," he said, gesturing behind him.

"Well, good luck." Tracy jammed her feet into her shoes and stood up. "I gotta go and check out what's happening in the back."

Relieved that Tyler had taken the first step towards mending the strained climate between them, Rayna felt some of the tension ease from her body. Smiling sheepishly, she said, "I hope you'll accept my apology. My behavior yesterday was inexcusable."

"It was my fault. I had no business pestering you."

"You weren't. I shouldn't have overreacted."

He waved away her protest. "It's okay. I didn't come here today to get you all riled up again. I just wanted to say goodbye to you in person."

She blinked in disbelief. "Goodbye?"

"Labor problems at the plant. I'm flying out tonight."

The unexpected pang of disappointment surprised her. Shouldn't she be happy to have a reprieve? With Tyler out of the picture her life would return to normal. And what was normal? Endless hours of work with one afternoon a week at the zoo, her exercise routine, a social event now and then with friends, and the occasional evening out once in a while in the company of a man who usually bored her to tears? "How ah…how long will you be away?"

"Hard to tell."

Before she could formulate a response, Tracy bounded up and grabbed her hand. "I'm really sorry, Rayna. I know I promised to give you a ride back, but I've got to stay here and help Mom for a couple more hours. I don't expect you to hang around waiting for me, so do you want me to have Paul drive you home?"

"If it's no inconvenience."

"I can give you a ride," Tyler offered, straining to maintain a matter-of-fact tone.

Rayna's pulse fluttered. Poised to decline, she stunned herself by saying, "I suppose that would be all right."

"Hey, super. See you later." Tracy winked at her before hurrying away.

Rayna turned to Tyler, eyeing him with amused suspicion. "You two didn't by any chance cook this up together, did you?"

Tyler assumed an air of bemusement. "Do you really think I would stoop to such tactics for the sole purpose of getting you alone?"

It was the way he lingered over the word 'alone' that sent a pleasurable chill clear through her bones. She could no longer stifle the smile that twitched at the corners of her mouth. "Indeed I do."

He rose, throwing his hands up in mock surrender. "Since I'm no match for your wits, Counselor, I reserve the right to remain silent about this matter. Ready to go?"

Even though she'd agreed to go with him, she still felt paralyzed by doubts. "I thought you wanted to bid on the cameras."

"I'm sure there will be others. I'll contact Tracy or her mother one of these days. I have her business card," he said, tapping his shirt pocket. "Okay?"

For long seconds, she sat in silence, waging an inner battle. In the deepest recesses of her heart, she had known from the moment their eyes met two days ago that she would eventually arrive at this dangerous crossroad.

She'd been here once before and could not escape the mental image of her past—a forlorn landscape littered with the sad remains of wrong decisions. Should she listen to the objections of her logical mind or surrender to the eager longing in her heart?

She looked up into his expectant brown eyes and smiled. "I'm ready to go."

Maintaining eye contact, he inclined his head. "Madam, your chariot awaits."

A cool breeze fluffed Rayna's hair as they left the antique shop and walked across the parking lot. She buttoned her short jacket, noting with satisfaction that the bank of clouds gathering above the western mountains promised a picture-perfect sunset.

But when they reached the late model Lincoln Town Car and Tyler opened the passenger door for her, the pounding of her heart unequivocally confirmed what she'd been trying so desperately to deny. Rooted to the spot, she struggled with the intuitive knowledge that if she accompanied him now, she would be inviting an irreversible change in her life.

"Won't you step into my parlor, said the spider to the fly," Tyler said with a playful grin and a broad sweep of his hand.

All at once, she felt as though she were two separate people. One, Deputy County Prosecutor Rayna Manchester bent on pressing the Brockwell case to conclusion; and the other was Rayna Daniels, the dreamy-eyed young woman reuniting with her first and only love. With the curtain of destiny parting before her, she blinked as if coming out of a trance and slid into the car.

Tyler drove on to the main road, not quite able to believe Rayna was really sitting beside him. After her contentious behavior yesterday, he was surprised and gratified that she had decided to set aside her misgivings and accompany him.

Last night things had seemed so bleak, so hopeless, as he'd lain awake in bed, reviewing all the impediments wedged between them. He'd tortured himself, picturing her in the arms of another man. He stole a glance at her, hoping she did not sense his eagerness. She looked serene. Was he alone in his feelings? He was tempted to ask about last night but forced himself to hold back. "Do you have to rush home?" he finally managed to ask. "I noticed a sign earlier indicating that there were some Indian ruins about ten miles east of here. Might be a good photo opportunity."

She shrugged. "Sure, that's fine."

"You know the lay of the land. Other than the ruins, what else would you suggest that wouldn't be too far out of the way?"

She considered his question for a moment before saying, "Well, Saguaro National Monument isn't too far." The instant the words left her mouth, she chastised herself. What about all the paperwork she needed to finish before work tomorrow? What was happening to her priorities?

In the enclosed intimate space, she was very aware of his nearness, the pleasing scent of his aftershave, the little tufts of hair curling on the back of his finely-shaped hands as they rested on the steering wheel. The thought of how they'd once caressed her, made her feel utterly vulnerable. Instinctively, she clutched the seat cushion when, without warning, he pulled to the side of the two lane road and stopped. Her pulse escalated when he turned to her, his face solemn, his dark eyes unreadable. He looked so unbelievably desirable, it was an effort not to reach out and touch him.

81

"Why did you stop?" she managed to whisper hoarsely.

"I'm hungry."

She blinked in surprise. "What?"

"I never had lunch. Did you?"

"Actually...no." She'd been so wired at the thought of seeing him again she'd eaten nothing since dinner the previous evening. And now, at the mention of food, her stomach rumbled. She pressed a hand to her abdomen, her cheeks blazing with embarrassment. A second later they broke into gales of laughter.

"Okay," Tyler said, still grinning as he checked for traffic and pulled back on the road, "Where would you suggest? I'm up for just about anything at this point."

Rayna dabbed tears from the corners of her eyes, feeling more lighthearted than she had in many years. "I'm not that familiar with this end of town, but I'm sure we'll find something."

A mile or so later, they exchanged an expectant glance as a sign loomed ahead. *Prickly Pete's Javelina Burgers—Best Barbequed Pork this side of the border.*

Tyler glanced at her, raising an expectant brow. "What do you think? Should we chance it?"

Rayna allowed herself to relax and enjoy the unexpected adventure. "Considering what javelinas look like," she said, scrunching her nose in distaste, "a burger made from one of those creatures doesn't sound particularly appetizing, but what the heck let's give it a shot."

Their enthusiasm quickly dissipated when they reached *Prickly Pete's* and found it closed, as was *Chuck Wagon Ribs* and *Hungry Man Diner* two and three miles later, respectively.

CHASING RAYNA

"I didn't realize so many places were closed on Sunday afternoon," Rayna sighed. "Let's turn around and get back on the freeway. There are a thousand places to eat along I-10."

"And miss all this great scenery?" With one eye on the road, Tyler scanned the folded map beside him, checked the route sign and made a sharp right. "I'll bet there's something further up ahead."

"I wouldn't bet on that, Tyler. This is Arizona," Rayna advised, challenging him with a good-natured grimace. "As in miles and miles of open desert?"

He flung the road map into the back seat and stepped on the gas. "In the true spirit of the western pioneers, I say we forge ahead and take whatever life hands us. Are you game?"

His devil-may-care spirit was intoxicating and contagious. Suddenly, she felt sixteen again and deliciously reckless. "All right, let's go for it!"

Tyler's quick glance before he returned his attention to the road held a glint of intimacy. "I like your hair worn loose like that."

"Thank you." She watched him press buttons on the radio and once again, questioned the wisdom of accepting his offer. Undoubtedly, she was barreling headlong into uncharted territory. Common sense told her she should ask him to take her home immediately, but any semblance of willpower seemed to have deserted her.

When he began to sing along with an old tune playing on the radio, the timbre of his resonant voice stirred up a host of memories she'd spent a lifetime trying to forget. She was overcome with an almost suffocating combination of pain and elation. A warning suddenly flashed in her mind's eye. *Beware! Don't let your guard*

SYLVIA NOBEL

down. But she stubbornly swept it aside. Life was too short. Hadn't she wasted enough time already?

There was so much living to do, so much beauty to enjoy, she thought, looking out the window at the cactus-covered landscape flying past. Straight ahead, the crooked pinnacles of rock jutting skyward into the vivid blue sky, struck a familiar chord. "I know where we are," she said, recognizing that they were traveling along the old state highway. "Chances of finding any place to eat along here are slim to none."

Tyler checked his watch and threw her a defiant look. "I'd be willing to wager that we'll find something in exactly five minutes."

"Oh, really. What's the wager?"

"Loser grants winner one wish."

The glow of desire in his eyes left no doubt in her mind that their wish would be the same. Nevertheless, she didn't dare convey her true feelings. "No dice. I don't wager unless I know the stakes in advance."

"Don't you?" he asked softly. His suggestive tone sent an icy sheet of goose bumps careening up her arms.

As they rounded a hairpin turn, a sign came into view. "Haus Dietermann's German Restaurant?" she mused aloud, relieved to change the subject. A faded red arrow directed them to turn right onto a gravel road. They'd traveled only a half a mile or so when Rayna's mouth dropped open in amazement. In a land of adobe, stucco, and rambling wooden ranch houses, the red and white chalet, perched on a gentle knoll, looked decidedly out of place.

Tyler tapped his watch triumphantly. "What did I tell you? Five minutes with thirty seconds to spare."

"Look at this place! It's like the gingerbread house in Hansel and Gretel. I wonder if it's still in business."

He swung onto the gravel road. "Only one way to find out."

Rayna leaned forward for a better look. To her right, a windmill graced the center of a rock garden overflowing with bright pink bougainvilleas and a sea of multi-colored wildflowers. And on her left, at least a dozen white ducks floated across an oval-shaped pond spanned by a gracefully arched stone footbridge. Enchanted, she thought the entire setting resembled a fairyland tucked away in the desert.

As Tyler slowed to a stop in the parking area, she marveled, "You know, I think I've heard of this place, but I didn't realize it was located so far from downtown." They shared a glance of relief at the OPEN sign in the window, where cheery pots of well-tended geraniums more than made up for the sight of peeling paint and the sagging roof of the outdoor patio which was sprinkled with a mishmash of chairs, tables and wooden picnic benches. Two signs, one reading *Wir wuenschen guten appetit!* and the second reading *Biergarten* rocked back and forth in the brisk afternoon breeze.

"Do you think we're properly dressed for such a grand place?" Tyler joked, tucking his plaid shirt snugly into his blue jeans and smoothing his ruffled hair into place.

Joining in the fun, she replied, "I'm positive the maitre d' will have a tie on hand for you." No sooner had they stepped from the car than she let out an exclamation of disappointment. "Oh, no!"

At the front window, a stern-looking woman in a flowered print dress was turning the sign to CLOSED.

When she looked up and saw them, her eyes widened with surprise. From behind the glass, she pointed to the sign and mouthed something.

Tyler watched with amusement as Rayna assumed an utterly forlorn expression and steepled her hands in an imploring gesture. "Please," she entreated, a few seconds later when the woman opened the front door, "won't you take pity on two starving people? If we could just get a couple of sandwiches, anything really, we'd be eternally grateful."

The woman appeared unmoved. "Ve always close at two," she stated gruffly with a distinct German accent. "But, vait here. I vill ask my husband. He does most of da cooking." After she'd turned and disappeared inside, Rayna turned expectantly to Tyler, her fingers crossed. "What do you think?"

Tyler's eyes twinkled with warmth. "I think it would be hard to resist someone as lovely and charming as you."

"Thank you," she murmured, locking eyes with him, unable to suppress the surge of happiness radiating through every inch of her body. A moment later, she heard the woman's voice behind her. "Okay, I talked with John. He vill make cold sandviches since you are already here."

"Madam, we are forever in your debt," Tyler said, taking full advantage of his southern drawl. Rayna was not surprised to see the woman's stern demeanor visibly thaw as he favored her with his infectious grin. Smiling in return, she beckoned to them. "Please, come in."

They followed her in the front door and she showed them to a small lace-draped table adjacent to the window overlooking the pond. "Vould you like sometink to drink?"

"Iced tea would be wonderful," Rayna replied, smiling up at her.

"Make that two," Tyler chimed in. "By the way, my name is Tyler Brockwell and this is Rayna Manchester."

She nodded politely in Rayna's direction, but reserved a sunny smile for Tyler. "My name is Rose Marie. I vill come back in a few minutes." Her shoes squeaked as she hurried across the hardwood floor and disappeared through the swinging door to the kitchen.

Rayna studied the restaurant's décor. It was immaculate, not a speck of dust on any of the hand-painted glassware displayed on the impressive mahogany sideboard or the marble mantelpiece above the fireplace. She felt Tyler's gaze on her as she admired the faded photographs of well-known European landmarks as well as an elaborately carved cuckoo clock.

"A penny for your thoughts," Tyler asked softly.

She leaned in and whispered confidentially, "I was just wondering how anyone could make a living running a restaurant out here along such a deserted stretch of road."

"I was thinking the exact same thing. Doesn't it make you feel like we took a wrong turn someplace back there and drove into an old episode of The Twilight Zone?"

She suppressed a giggle as Rose returned with frosty glasses of iced tea topped with lemon wedges, and then set out silverware and napkins, all the while humming a little tune.

"How do people find your place?" Tyler inquired politely.

"The same vay you did. If ve get a handful of customers a day, dat's a lot. Business vas good until the new freeway vas built. Now it is mostly vord of mouth."

SYLVIA NOBEL

"How do you afford to stay open?" he asked with genuine concern.

She shrugged. "Ve are open for lunch during da veek and for dinner on Friday and Saturday only. John loves to cook and it gives him sometink to stay busy." At the sharp ring of a bell, she hurried to the kitchen, returning promptly accompanied by a stocky man with abundant white hair and twinkling blue eyes. As they set the plates of food on the table, Rose introduced her husband and they all exchanged names once again.

"Thank you both for your kindness. This is magnificent," Rayna cried, clapping her hands together as she eyed the towering turkey and ham sandwiches made with dark pumpernickel bread, accompanied by a sizeable mound of hot German potato salad and the biggest dill pickle she'd ever seen. She and Tyler finished every bite and were overwhelmed when the couple reappeared with thick wedges of hot apple strudel topped with generous dips of vanilla ice cream.

A half hour later Rayna pushed away from the table with a groan. "I don't think I've ever eaten so much in my life."

"I'm with you there," Tyler agreed, slipping a generous tip beneath the bill. Rising to leave, they showered praise on John and Rose for the impromptu feast and their hospitality. Each of them happily accepted several copies of the menu and promised to return one day.

Outside, Tyler persuaded everyone to pose for photographs in front of the house. He snapped several of the smiling couple with Rayna squeezed between them. After a flurry of goodbyes, Rose suggested that they tour the grounds before returning to Tucson.

88

After the older pair had gone inside, Tyler shot Rayna a questioning look and gestured towards the garden. "What do you think? Have you got time to take them up on their offer?"

"Sure. I guess so," she said, falling into step with him as they walked past the *Biergarten*. Eyeing the checkered red and white tablecloths, it was easy to imagine the place in its heyday, full of people, singing, toasting with their beer steins, and perhaps even dancing to the energetic beat of a polka.

They crossed to the garden surrounding the pond, and paused to admire the flowers and watch the ducks gliding around each other, quacking softly. Rayna took a deep breath filled with contentment and hope. But by the same token, she felt a sense of profound regret that this moment could not be frozen in time forever.

Tyler watched her walk ahead to stand on the curved footbridge. She rested her arms on the railing, her gaze resting dreamily on the water. For the first time since their paths had crossed, she appeared to be carefree. He felt as though he were looking through a window into the past, as though he were seeing her nineteen years ago, a blossoming, innocent girl full of life, full of optimism, exploring an untarnished world.

He drank in the sight of her—the dark halo of hair framing her oval face, her slender neck and the sensuous swell of her breasts. His eyes trailed down to her slim waist, on to the voluptuous curve of her hips and finally to her shapely legs. He longed to touch her. This was no fantasy, no vision from the past, but the living, breathing woman who'd pervaded his feverish dreams. All at once, long-sequestered emotions that had tortured his soul for an eternity craved release. He moved towards her as if summoned by an inexplicable force and stood beside her, his skin burning, his heart hammering hard against his ribs.

"Look at all those colors. Aren't they gorgeous?" she murmured, pointing to the school of Koi fish swirling beneath the surface of the sun-dappled water like plump iridescent rainbows.

Tyler nodded in agreement, then fixed his eyes on Rayna once more. He was tempted to say that they paled before her beauty. He ached to tell her that he'd never stopped loving her, but could not find the right words. Tentatively, he slid his hand over hers and held his breath. To his delight, she did not protest. Instead, her fingers curled around his.

"Rayna..." he whispered. The blood pounded through his veins as he dipped his head and lightly skimmed her lips. He drew back and looked deep into her amazing violet eyes, seeking permission. Sudden euphoria flooded him at the light of invitation reflected in them. Her parted lips drew him like a magnet. This time when he kissed her, it was with all the urgency and desperation of a lost wanderer who, after surviving a lifetime in a merciless desert, had at last come to an oasis, had at last come home.

CHAPTER SEVEN

In the subdued light of her plant-draped bathroom, Rayna stepped into the tub and sighed contentedly as she slipped beneath the fragrant blanket of bubbles. Eyes half closed, she rested her head against the bath pillow and luxuriated in the warm water. She lay still for a few moments, allowing the soothing heat to infuse every pore of her skin, then reached for the bar of scented soap and slowly circled it around her breasts and down her belly as she relived Tyler's impassioned kiss. She'd been startled when his lips had tentatively touched hers. But when he'd pulled away, the sudden urge to return his kiss was so intense, so desperate, all of her reservations simply evaporated.

A searing tingle centered in her body as she once again experienced the erotic sensations his sensuous kiss had awakened in her. Perhaps it was her impassioned state of mind that released the flow of memories she'd kept carefully locked away for so long. Little by little the mist that obscured the past dissipated like clouds scattering in the wind, revealing vivid recollections: joyful recollections of her humble home, rich with caring and devotion; of her mother's gentle strength, of dear sweet Adam, and the strong bond she shared with her father. And she remembered every detail of the day Tyler had come into her life.

How could she have forgotten the way he'd lovingly held her hand at the county fair, their first kiss at the top of the Ferris wheel, or her giddy exhilaration when

91

he chased her across the flower-filled meadow by the river? He'd caught her and wrestled her to the ground, where, with the blue sky above as the sole witness, he'd tenderly made love to her. She felt as though she'd at last awakened from a long, troubled sleep, and for the first time in years a warm glow of happiness filled her entire being.

He'd been gone less than two hours, yet she already missed him. He'd kissed her goodbye at the door and whispered, "I'll call you tomorrow," before hurrying away to catch his flight.

With a little sigh, Rayna reluctantly stepped out, pulled a bath towel from the rack and began to dry off. She stared at her reflection in the mirror and knew for certain there was no choice but to take the path dictated by her heart. First thing in the morning, she would speak with Mitchell and withdraw from the Brockwell case.

***

As though an oppressive weight had been lifted from her chest, Rayna strode purposefully across the sun-splashed marble floor of the court building and stepped onto the escalator. Her decision last night would by no means solve all her problems, but she was not about to second-guess it. There were several difficult hurdles still awaiting her and plenty of loose ends to tie up. Her withdrawal would prompt curious speculation from her colleagues as well as the press. Then there was still the ordeal of Scott's trial to endure, whether she was directly involved or not. But how could she not be, given that he was Tyler's son?

But regardless of how the case turned out, she could soon be faced with another decision. Depending on when

Tyler's divorce became final, could she, if he should ask her, forsake her hard-earned reputation and leave Arizona to start over in South Carolina with him? There was no point in broaching the question in reverse. She knew Tyler would never consider leaving the business his father had left him. Impatiently, she forced down the disquieting thoughts. The best course of action was to take one step at a time. She would get the ball rolling by informing Mitchell of her decision to relinquish the case.

She opened the door to the reception area and glanced up at the clock. "Damn," she muttered under her breath. The bold black numbers confirmed that she was a full half hour late. She called a hasty greeting over her shoulder to the receptionist and hurried down the corridor.

Charging through the doorway of her office, Rayna waved at Miguel, who interrupted his phone conversation long enough to return her greeting. After setting the stack of files on her desk, she dropped into the chair and took a few seconds to catch her breath.

"So, did you get caught up in that freeway accident this morning?" Miguel inquired, hanging up the phone.

"Nope. I was up late and slept in."

"Pretty busy weekend, huh?"

"It sure was. I'm so far behind I'll probably be here until late this evening."

"Rats," he said, frowning. "I was hoping you could fill in for me at an IA this morning. I've got to take Angelina to the doctor at ten."

Rayna skimmed her finger down the calendar. "Go ahead. I guess I can squeeze it in."

"Thanks." Without another word, he grabbed the miniature basketball off the filing cabinet behind him and sank it into the small net on the adjacent wall. He continued shooting hoops in uncharacteristic silence until Rayna looked up from her desk. "Miguel, is there something bothering you?"

He swiveled to face her. "I just want to know one thing. Why was Tyler Brockwell at the zoo on Saturday?"

Her stomach jumped. "Are you going to give me a lecture?"

"Look. I'm not your father or your brother, but I *am* your friend and I'd sure as hell hate to see you get trapped in an ethical crossfire."

"You don't have to worry about that," she replied softly. "I'm taking myself off the case."

His eyes widened in surprise. "When did you decide that?"

"Yesterday."

"I wondered how long it would take you to realize what I knew the first minute I saw you two together."

"Are you waiting for me to say you're right as usual?"

He grinned mischievously. "Yeah. I want to hear you say it. It does my heart good to hear you admit how brilliantly perceptive I am."

Rayna shook her head. "How can Angelina stand to live with such a know-it-all?"

He laughed. "What can I say? It's a gift."

"So, do you want it?" she challenged.

"Want what?"

"The Brockwell case. If you do, I can mention it to Mitchell. I'm going to see him right now," she said, rising from her chair.

"Thanks to you I'm already too close to it. And you might as well sit back down because Mitchell isn't here. He's in Washington until Friday, remember?"

"Oh, I forgot." She settled into her chair again. "I assume that Tyler already knows about your decision?"

"Actually, no. He had to fly back to South Carolina for a business meeting. But I plan to tell him at the first opportunity."

He arched a brow. "No regrets?"

"None." She said it without the slightest hesitation.

"Okay, then. If you're happy, I'm happy." He rose and headed for the door. "Gotta run. Catch you later."

"You too." After he'd gone, Rayna eyed the phone, willing it to ring. She wondered what Tyler's reaction would be when she broke the news to him. But then, it occurred to her that it might be better to wait and tell him in person. Yes, that would be better. She'd tell him the moment he returned.

*　*　*

It was still dark when Tyler arrived back at the Marriott hotel in Tucson on Friday morning. He could hear the soft tinkling of glassware and the murmur of voices as he passed the coffee shop. Catching a whiff of freshly brewed coffee, he was almost tempted to run in and have a cup, but he resisted. Even though he'd managed to get an earlier flight, he would barely have time to shower and shave before the breakfast meeting with Sheldon and Scott. More importantly, he wanted to save a few minutes to call Rayna.

He'd only been able to have two agonizingly brief conversations with her during the four days he'd been gone. Trying to stay focused on the business at hand with his attorneys and the union leaders during the intense negotiations had been no easy task considering he could not stop thinking about the time they'd spent together Sunday afternoon.

His pulse raced wildly every time he thought of her sensuous body pressed against him. Neither of them had said much on the drive back, yet he could tell by the way she looked at him that something magical was happening between them. He'd been so anxious to wrap up his business and get back to Tucson that he'd worked practically around the clock. Happily, each side had agreed to the terms he'd felt comfortable with and the impending strike at the plant had been averted.

He glanced at the big clock in the lobby as he waited for the elevator. Five-forty-five—too early to call her. The sun wasn't even up yet. Feeling the strain of the past four days, coupled with the few fitful hours he'd slept on his flight, he massaged the back of his neck as he made his way down the carpeted hallway to his room. He let himself in and tossed his coat over the back of the sofa, before peeking into the second bedroom. The perfectly made bed revived his growing suspicion that Scott had not spent the previous night in his room. So where was he spending his nights? After several unsuccessful attempts to contact him regarding Sheldon's request to meet with both of them this morning, he'd finally reached him at his work number late yesterday afternoon.

Mystified by his son's puzzling behavior, he strode into his own room and dropped his garment bag onto the bed. It bothered him greatly that Scott was so secretive concerning his whereabouts and his friends. And where the hell was he now? Tyler could no longer push aside the dark thoughts plaguing him. There were a lot of things that didn't add up. It was time to have a serious talk with him.

CHASING RAYNA

He dug his shaving kit from the bag and entered the bathroom. He'd call Rayna as soon as he finished showering. Thinking of her helped relieve the unsettling sensation invading his stomach. Would she have time to meet him for lunch? That thought prompted him to retrace his steps to the closet. He paused to contemplate what he would wear and finally chose the new navy polo shirt. The gold Movado watch he'd purchased the same day would complement it. He couldn't help smiling to himself. It had been years since he'd taken such pains with his appearance. He opened the top drawer of the bureau and blinked in surprise. The box containing the new watch was gone. A careful search of every drawer produced nothing. The most likely explanation jumped out at him. One of the maids had swiped it. But then his gaze fell on the case containing his new Nikon camera and expensive lenses that he'd left on top of his bureau. They were worth far more than the watch.

Deeply troubled, he headed for the shower. Ten minutes later, as he briskly dried off, Tyler tried to fend off the cold despair gathering in his gut. If it wasn't one of the maids, then there remained only one obvious suspect. Scott. He tossed the towel towards the counter, but missed. It hit the waste can instead, scattering the contents onto the tile floor. Sighing in exasperation, he bent to retrieve them, only to stop and stare in surprise at a plastic container of purple eye shadow. As he turned it over in his hand, he felt a jab of disappointment. His son was by no means perfect, but he'd never before known him to be a liar. So he did have a girlfriend. Then, why the subterfuge? Tyler shook off his glum mood and strode into the living room to call Rayna. She should be up by now, he thought, watching the first rays of sunlight stream through the window. He needed to hear her voice. Just as he reached for the phone, the door opened and Scott walked in, his startled expression conveying more than simple surprise. "Dad! I...ah. I thought your plane didn't get in until after seven."

"I caught an earlier flight."

Scott jammed his hands into his front pockets and hunched his shoulders in obvious discomfort. "Well...um...welcome back."

"Thanks. You're certainly up and out early. I was beginning to wonder if you'd forgotten about meeting with Sheldon this morning."

"I'm here, aren't I?"

"But you haven't been here much lately, have you?"

"I gotta grab a shower." Scott breezed past him.

"Hang on a minute," Tyler called out after him. "Did you borrow my new watch?"

Scott swung around, scowling. "No."

"I see. Well then, perhaps your friend borrowed it?"

Scott stared at him. "What are you talking about?"

"Don't play games with me. I know you had a visitor while I was gone." Tyler watched carefully for some reaction, but Scott's expression remained stoic.

"Nobody else was here but me."

Tyler suppressed the flare of anger. "You're positive about that?"

"What's that supposed to mean? You think I'm lying?" he grumbled, unable to maintain eye contact with his father.

"I would have never thought so before, but perhaps you'd care to explain this." When he held up the container of eye shadow, the flash of raw panic in Scott's eyes was all he needed. "Why don't you just tell the truth? And while you're at it, I'd like to know where you're spending your nights when you're not here. You told me you were staying at a motel before the accident."

Scott's eyes narrowed. "In case you forgot, I'm almost nineteen. You can't tell me what to do anymore. Where I go and what I do is none of your business."

Tyler thundered, "Your irresponsible behavior has damn well made it my business! And I wasn't born yesterday. It's apparent that you're hiding something."

Scott's expression turned sly. "I guess we all hide things sometimes, don't we, Dad?"

Tyler frowned. "What are you talking about?"

"Right. Like you don't know."

The sudden jangle of the telephone startled both of them. Mystified by Scott's remark, Tyler lifted the receiver at the same instant Scott slammed the door to his room.

"I'm downstairs in the coffee shop," Sheldon Freestone announced tersely.

"We'll be right there." Tyler hung up and ran a weary hand over his forehead. What was happening? His life seemed to be careening out of control. He marched to Scott's room and pounded on the door, shouting, "Freestone's downstairs!"

"You can both go to hell," came Scott's muffled retort.

Tyler prayed for patience. "Come on, son, be realistic," he said, lowering his voice. "This kind of behavior isn't going to help either of us. We'll be waiting for you."

Twenty minutes later Scott sauntered into the restaurant and slumped wordlessly into a chair. Tyler bit back the words of recrimination crowding his throat and said to Sheldon, "You talk to him. Maybe he'll listen to you."

Freestone slid each of them a shrewd glance, then popped the last bite of buttered toast into his mouth while the waiter cleared away the empty plates. Once he was out of earshot, Sheldon repeated what he'd already discussed with Tyler, carefully explaining the legal technicalities that lay ahead. The rising irritation in his voice indicated that he was more than a little annoyed by Scott's indifferent behavior. "I don't think you fully appreciate how much trouble you're in."

"Wait a minute. You told me I'd probably only get probation," Scott challenged, his tone petulant.

Freestone's eyes narrowed in annoyance. "I said you *might*, and that's only because you have no prior arrests. Listen to me. If that woman and her little girl take a turn for the worse, you're toast. We won't be dealing with just aggravated assault. We could be looking at manslaughter or even second-degree murder. Do you understand what I'm saying to you? There's a very real possibility you could go to prison, so I'd suggest you undergo an attitude adjustment starting right now."

Tyler watched Scott shift in his chair and fold his arms tightly against his chest. For the first time since his arrival, he detected tangible alarm in the young man's eyes. "Man, you're not serious?" There was a ring of false bravado in his tone.

"We can't ignore the possibility," Freestone said gravely. "And with that in mind, it might help to have a little more cooperation from your end. Your father seems to think you may have some information you're not sharing with us. If it's pertinent to the case, I suggest you tell us what it is without delay."

Scott appeared to be weighing something as he fiddled with the silverware. "I already told you everything," he mumbled, averting his eyes.

Tyler met Freestone's dubious glance and gave him a slight shake of his head.

"You'd better be telling us the truth, young man," Freestone snapped impatiently. "The powers that be in this town are out for blood and you have no idea how much shit is going to rain down on you. It's no help having Rayna Manchester prosecuting this case. That lady's got one of the best conviction records in the entire county. Believe me, if you're not leveling with us, she'll have you for breakfast in that courtroom."

"Maybe Dad can put in a good word for me," Scott announced with an undertone of sarcasm.

Tyler drew back, perplexed by his son's vindictive tone and secretive smile. "What are you talking about?"

Scott pulled two photos from his shirt pocket and slapped them down on the table. "Maybe these will help you get the picture, so to speak."

Freestone's thick brows knotted in surprise. One snapshot was of Rayna at the zoo and the second showed her standing with the Dietermanns in front of their restaurant.

"Where in the hell did you get these?" Tyler demanded, his face flushing.

Scott rocked back in his chair, looking smug. "From the concierge. You gave him the rolls of film to be developed before you left, remember?"

Tyler felt a blaze of outrage. "Where do you come off opening my...."

"You know Rayna Manchester?" Freestone interrupted incredulously, tapping the photos with his index finger. "Why didn't you say so?"

"I didn't think it would make any difference one way or the other. We grew up in the same town twenty years ago and I just happened to bump into her after the hearing." He knew his explanation didn't even begin to explain the photos and he didn't miss the speculative gleam in Sheldon Freestone's eyes.

"I'm late for work," Scott said, jumping to his feet, clearly pleased that he'd shifted the spotlight to his father. He started for the exit but hadn't gone three feet when Freestone's gruff voice stopped him. "Come back here."

Wheeling around, he slouched back to the table, narrowing his eyes at the indignant attorney. "What?"

Freestone's eyes flashed fire and he crooked his finger for Scott to come closer. "Listen to me, young man," he snarled through gritted teeth, "for your own sake, I suggest you begin working on your tarnished image. You can start by wiping that insufferable smirk off your face and think about how you're going to appear before a jury. I'm going to be out of town until Thursday of next week. Between now and then, I advise that you give some serious thought to what you might have forgotten to tell us about this case. Are we clear?"

"Uh-huh." Scott edged him a sidelong glance before strolling out of the coffee shop.

Tyler cleared his throat. "Sheldon, before you go, I want to clarify my relationship with Rayna Manchester...."

Freestone grabbed his briefcase and rose. "No need. I'm late for a meeting with another client at the moment, but you can be sure we'll discuss this soon."

***

The knowledge that Tyler would be back in town that day added an extra spring to Rayna's step as she walked out of the courtroom and hurried towards her office. Her unrestrained joy must have been evident, judging by the receptive smiles from colleagues and strangers she encountered along the way. Adding to her sense of well-being was the prospect of informing Mitchell of her decision to conflict off. She swept into her office, humming, and gave Miguel an elated smile.

"I can tell your morning went well," he said, looking up from his desk.

"So far." She set her briefcase down beside her chair and removed her beige suit jacket. "Anything exciting happening here?" she asked, thumbing through the stack of messages near her telephone.

"That's anybody's guess."

"Hmmm. How mysterious," she said absently. "What does that mean?"

"Mitchell wants to see you."

"Good. That makes two of us. I've been waiting all week to get this off my chest." She met his gaze. "Do you know what he wants?"

"No. But, something's not good. When he stuck his head in here a couple of hours ago, he was breathing fire."

"Fire, huh?" she repeated absently, her heart jumping with delight as she read the two messages from Tyler asking her to call his hotel as soon as possible.

"Did you hear what I said?"

"Yes, yes. I'll see him in a minute," she said, reaching for the receiver. "I have to make one quick call first."

"You're still not listening," Miguel said grimly. "Judging by the expression on Mitchell's face, I'd advise you to go see him pronto."

Rayna shot him a puzzled look and cradled the phone.

"Sounds pretty heavy. Do you have any idea what it could be?"

"I didn't ask."

Hurrying towards Mitchell's office, her curiosity was exceeded only by her apprehension. In all the years he'd been her boss, she'd never known him to be anything but even-tempered. Something serious must have happened on the trip to Washington D.C. She rapped lightly on his door before opening it a crack and peeking in. Mitchell looked up from his desk and motioned for her to enter and sit down. His solemn face set off a series of little alarm bells inside her as she gingerly slid into the upholstered leather chair opposite him. "Welcome back," she said with a hesitant smile.

His cold stare made her feel like a little girl who'd been called into the principal's office. "I got a disturbing call from Sheldon Freestone this morning."

Fifteen minutes later, Rayna quietly closed Mitchell's door and stood in the hallway leaning against it for support. Her entire body was trembling. She pressed a fist against her lips to stifle the sobs of humiliation rising in her throat as Mitchell's harsh words of recrimination rang in her ears. 'Why didn't you tell me you knew the defendant's father? Freestone told me that you and Tyler Brockwell are more than just acquaintances and he has the photos to prove it.' Unable to refute his statement, she'd sat in stunned silence as Mitchell expressed his disappointment at her lack of discretion and lectured her on the ethical ramifications of her actions. How could Tyler have done something so evil, so wretched? How could she have believed that he cared for her when all the while he'd been planning to deceive her? She should have heeded the lessons of the past. He had taken advantage of her loneliness, cleverly ingratiated himself for the sole purpose of forcing her off the case. What an idiot she'd been! She'd allowed her stupid, naïve, gullible heart to mislead her again. What excuse could she offer herself this time? She was no longer the innocent, inexperienced girl who'd fallen victim to his charms the first time. She was a mature woman with few illusions, a prosecutor who'd seen more than her share of deception and manipulation in the day-to-day exchange with the seamier side of life. And in spite of all the training and skepticism, she'd let her guard down.

Oh, you're good, Tyler Brockwell! Damn good! Not only had he charmed his way back into her life, he'd methodically set her up with incriminating photographs for good measure, handing Freestone the ammunition to undermine her position with Mitchell. He'd been relentless, perpetuating the charade, phoning her from Summersville to tell her how much he missed her, how he could hardly wait to see her. And the messages he'd left her this morning—as though nothing were wrong. Somehow, she willed her legs to carry her back to the office. Collapsing in her chair, she vacantly stared at the folders on her desk.

"*¡Dios mio!* What happened in there?" Miguel cried. "You look like someone just died."

"I can't believe that bastard..." her words faltered as she blinked back tears.

"Whoa! Are you talking about Mitchell?"

"No! Tyler Brockwell. He got me thrown off the case."

Miguel's eyebrows shot up. "Say what?"

"He used me, Miguel, went behind my back...I believed him! I thought...."

"Would you stop babbling and start at the beginning."

Between angry sobs, she poured her heart out to him and confessed her feelings for Tyler—then and now.

His ruddy complexion flushing red with emotion, he dramatically smacked his palm on the desk. "Crap! I was afraid of that. I knew you were going to get hurt."

She angrily swiped at the tears streaming down her cheeks. "And the worst part is, I should have known better."

Miguel jumped up, closed the door and moved to her side, placing a comforting hand on her shoulder. "Why don't you go home early? I'll explain it to Mitchell."

She shook her head. "He told me to take the afternoon off. Oh, my God! Can you imagine what's going to happen when the press gets wind of this?"

"Then what are you waiting for?" he cried, gesturing towards the door. "Go! In fact, why don't you just pack a bag and go someplace quiet for the weekend where you can get your head together."

Rayna dabbed at her eyes and nose. "I should go somewhere and have my head *examined*. Tyler lied to me before and I should have known better. Why didn't I see it coming? I mean...I'm a halfway intelligent person, aren't I? Instead, I've been acting like a love-struck teenager."

"Don't be so hard on yourself. Better that you found out sooner than later. Forget about him."

"Can you believe he had the nerve to call this morning?" she raged, tearing the phone messages into smithereens. "I wonder what lies he planned to tell me. How much he missed me? How much he cares for me?"

"You know, my sister has a casita in Mexico," Miguel began softly. "Very secluded. No TV, no phone, no fax, nothing. And your cell phone won't work there either. Sound interesting?"

Rayna forced a few deep breaths and looked up into his sympathetic brown eyes. "Where is it?"

"Lake Bonita. She offered it to us this weekend, but we can't travel with Angelina being so late in her pregnancy."

Rayna fell silent as she mulled over his offer.

"Hey," Miguel said with a defensive shrug when she didn't respond. "Just an idea."

"Please don't think I don't appreciate it. The thought of getting away, of leaving this whole mess behind me sounds wonderful, but I can't. I'd be doing the same thing I did before. I'd be running away again."

"I fail to see the comparison. You're only going away for the weekend, for Pete's sake. Do yourself a favor. Go pack a swimsuit and a toothbrush."

Rayna gave Miguel a weak smile. He was right. She needed to go someplace where she wouldn't have to contend with anyone, especially Tyler. If it were up to her, she'd be just as happy to drop off the face of the earth. But since that wasn't possible, Lake Bonita sounded like the next best thing.

CHAPTER NINE

Tyler paced back and forth across the hotel room, his agitation increasing by the minute. Rayna should have returned his calls by now. Even if she'd been tied up in court all day as she'd forewarned, wouldn't she have checked her messages by now? He glanced at the clock for the umpteenth time. It was three-thirty. A persistent premonition of trouble had hung over him all afternoon. He'd been a fool to hope that Freestone would keep his mouth shut until he could explain to Rayna what had happened at breakfast. There was no point in leaving her another message. He grabbed the phone and punched in the numbers. "This is Tyler Brockwell," he said as soon as Miguel Castillo answered. "Sorry to bother you, but I've been trying to reach Rayna all day. Do you know where she is?"

"Nope, can't help you."

Tyler suppressed his annoyance at the man's curt reply. "Doesn't she usually check for messages?"

"Yep."

Miguel's aloof tone confirmed his worst fears. She knew about the photographs. "I need to speak with her, it's very important."

"It ain't going to happen, buddy."

"Listen, I didn't have anything to do with...."

"Yeah, right. You and Freestone can go throw yourselves a party now because she's off the case."

"Oh, my God. I have to talk to her."

"Well, you know what? She doesn't want to talk to you."

As the dial tone hummed in his ear, Tyler felt as though an iron fist was crushing his heart. He threw the phone down and bolted for the door. He drove towards her condo like a madman, only to find himself mired in rush-hour traffic. Fuming and cursing, he pulled out his cell phone and dialed her home number. Fat chance she'd answer since she'd recognize his number immediately. How was he going to make this right?

By the time he finally reached her condo, the sun was sliding behind the distant mountain peaks, leaving a brilliant haze of scarlet and purple clouds in its wake. Rather than wait for the elevator, he sprinted up three flights of stairs and by the time he reached her door, his head was pounding and his throat was so dry it was difficult to swallow. When she didn't answer after the second ring, he knocked aggressively, calling out, "Rayna! I need to talk to you!"

"Can I help you?" came Mrs. Ansel's shout from across the hall. He wheeled around and hurried towards her. "Mr. Brockwell!" the old woman gasped, recognition dawning in her eyes, "I didn't realize it was you."

Cold apprehension settled in his stomach when he noticed Beauregarde in her arms. He forced a smile. "Delighted to see you again, Mrs. Ansel."

Her color heightened. "And, it's lovely to see you again."

Tyler looked over her head through the open doorway. "I'm looking for Rayna. We…I thought we were going to see each other this evening."

Mrs. Ansel's eyes clouded in confusion. "Well, mercy me. I don't understand. That doesn't sound like her.

But," she added, her tone turning confidential, "she did seem a little upset this afternoon. She said she had a bad day at work. I suppose you can expect to have bad days when you have to deal with the criminal element all day long, day after day. Eldon, that was my late husband, he owned some rental property and I remember going to court with him because of one of his tenants owed him...."

"Do you know where she is?" Tyler cut in, still smiling while trying hard to remain calm.

"She went away for the weekend. She took the airport shuttle several hours ago."

Tyler stared at her, uncomprehending, for a few seconds. "Did she tell you where she was going?"

"Of course," she said, scratching Beauregarde's chin. "She went to Mexico."

"Mexico?" he asked incredulously.

Her eyes sparkled with humor. "Don't look so surprised, dear. It's really not all that far away from here. People pop down there and back all the time. I can remember a time when...."

Tyler prayed for patience. "I assume that she told you where she'll be staying?"

"Well, of course she did." She tilted her head to one side, her smile secretive. "But, I'm not supposed to say."

Tyler's spirits sank like a rock. He'd done just what he feared most, screwed up his chance to win Rayna's trust. "I understand. I'm sorry to have bothered you." He turned to leave, but stopped when Mrs. Ansel gently inquired, "Did you two have a lover's quarrel?"

The lady was delightfully old-fashioned. Tyler grinned sheepishly. "I guess you could say that."

She nodded sagely. "I thought so. Young man, I just made a batch of fresh cookies and a pot of tea. Would you like to come in and have a cup with me?"

Tyler inclined his head. "I can't think of anything I would like better."

An hour later he was back in his car, and by the time he'd reached the hotel, his mind was made up. There was only one thing for him to do.

***

Rayna sat at a small table near the outer edge of the flagstone patio that graced the front entrance to the charming pink stucco hotel. Absently, she ran a finger around the salt-encrusted rim of the margarita glass and stared out into the smooth blue water of Lake Bonita. It was her second drink of the evening and she was finally beginning to feel the effects. Gradually, the tension began to ease from her shoulders and she welcomed the carefree sensation the tangy drink afforded her. Besides that, it helped dull the sharp ache of loneliness that filled her as she glanced around at the happy, chattering families and smiling, handholding couples seated at the other tables.

She could easily feel sorry for herself if she allowed it. For several years following Thomas's death, she'd hated the idea of dining alone, shopping alone and traveling alone. But gradually, she'd grown to enjoy the freedom of being single and doing whatever she pleased, whenever she pleased. So, why did she suddenly feel like a solitary bookend sitting on a shelf? With a despondent sigh, she pushed the thought from her mind, focusing instead on the wild beauty of the volcanic peaks set against a lavender-hued sky. Tall coconut palms rustled in a soft breeze that carried faint strains of guitar music from somewhere nearby.

Her lips curved whimsically as she took another sip of her margarita. A few hours ago she'd been in a crowded courtroom and now it was as though she'd been transported to an exotic movie set, and the effects were soothing and therapeutic. It was the perfect escape. As much as she hated to admit it, she was guilty of doing exactly that. Escaping. It galled her to think that the same man held the power to make her turn tail and run. Twice.

But hadn't her therapist drilled into her that no one holds power over another person unless that person allows it? She blinked back the hot tears stinging her eyelids. Wasn't that precisely what she had done, awarded Tyler the power to devastate her again? She tried to chase away the distressing thoughts, but her grief persisted. How could she have been so foolish, so blind? She had blithely accepted his false display of love while eagerly responding to his counterfeit kisses.

Enough! She pushed away from the table with the full knowledge that she was not the first woman to suffer from a broken heart and certainly wouldn't be the last. But she was a realist. More than that, she was a survivor. It would take time, but she would recover, starting right now. She mentally thanked Miguel again for his kindness and prayed that the much-needed solitude in this little piece of paradise would help heal her battered soul.

She felt slightly dizzy as she rose, and paused for a moment to get her bearings. Then she picked up her straw hat and strolled along a narrow path that crossed the center courtyard leading to her secluded casita. Her gauzy skirt brushed against bright orange and yellow tropical flowers, and when she stopped to inhale their pungent fragrance, she tried to objectively analyze her feelings, tried to understand why she'd been so affected by Tyler's persistence. In many ways, he'd always been with her, hovering at the periphery of her unconscious mind, holding her heart hostage, never allowing her to freely give it to another. And when he'd burst into her world a second time, she'd let down her guard and accepted it as a fitting resolution to her lifelong yearning.

In spite of the numbing sense of melancholy, Rayna vowed to exercise her inner strength and dwell on the one positive outcome of this unfortunate fiasco—that she would once and for all evict Tyler Brockwell from her heart. She must never look back.

As she rounded the corner of the hotel, the stillness was suddenly interrupted by the blare of trumpets. She paused and listened with delight as a band of Mariachis broke into song, welcoming a festive throng of people to the grassy courtyard where huge colorful paper-flower centerpieces topped a dozen banquet tables. A large banner stretched across a lattice-domed gazebo decorated with ribbons and balloons, boldly announced the occasion: *Boda de Maria y Francisco.* She recognized the Spanish word for wedding at the same instant she saw the radiant bride and groom posing with family for photographs and stealing kisses in between.

Eyes misty, a lump forming in her throat, Rayna turned to leave when a buxom woman in a bright scarlet dress seated at a nearby table waved at her. *"¡Venga!"* the woman beckoned enthusiastically with an ear-to-ear grin lighting her moon-shaped face. Unsure as to what she was saying, Rayna smiled and shrugged her confusion. The woman said something to two young girls in frilly dresses and they came running to her side. Giggling, they took her hands and pulled her to the table.

A chair was quickly unfolded for her and a frosty glass of sangria pressed into her hand. Feeling slightly ill at ease and unable to bridge the language barrier, she nevertheless felt a sense of gratitude that she, a total stranger, had been invited to join the festive celebration. She was escorted to a buffet table laden with mounds of savory Mexican food. Her glass was refilled again and again, and even after she protested, a merry group of revelers swept her onto the dance floor. Gradually, she began to shed her inhibitions and was soon gyrating to the lusty Latin beat. During the hours that followed, there was more cheering, more dancing and more toasts to the bride and groom. Rayna joined in the merriment, abandoning her worries and eagerly allowing herself to be absorbed into the joyous, carnival-like atmosphere.

***

It was mid-morning by the time Rayna cautiously opened her eyes and squinted at her watch. She closed them again quickly. The brilliant sunlight streaming in between flimsy flowered drapes stung her eyes and set up a dull throbbing in her head. She groaned and buried her face in the pillow, unable to clearly remember how the evening had ended or even how she'd managed to find her casita. For a while she lay perfectly still, until the cold sensation in her stomach and the pounding in her temples subsided, before easing to a sitting position. Okay. Given a few more minutes to recover, she might actually be able to stand.

CHASING RAYNA

Little by little a parade of hazy visions flashed through her mind. She recalled joining in a hearty chorus of *"mas, mas,* more more!" every time the zealous waiter refilled the empty pitchers of sangria. Vaguely, she remembered digging into indistinguishable platters of food swimming in tomato and cheese sauce, dominated by a fiery jalapeno salsa that scorched her throat. And then there was the dancing....

One particular scene crystallized in her thoughts. Feeling deliciously intoxicated, and encouraged by her enthusiastic tablemates, she'd been persuaded to join the professional dancers on the circular stage. Caught up in the excitement of the music, the cheers and applause, she'd strutted her stuff, imitating the can-can-like moves of the dancers flourishing their multi-layered petticoats. "Oh, no!" she whispered aloud, sliding a rueful glance at her sheer white skirt lying in a heap on the floor. Unfortunately, she hadn't had the advantage of the petticoats. Imagining the spectacle she must have presented set her cheeks on fire. She fervently prayed that she wouldn't run into any of the wedding guests during the remainder of her visit.

Confident that she could walk, she rose and padded to the bathroom. Revived by the ice cold shower, she donned a T-shirt and shorts. On a mission to find some strong, black coffee, she made her way along the brick walkway through the garden to the snack bar by the pool. Even with the benefit of dark glasses, the sun's rays seemed blindingly white, the sky piercingly blue, and the soft chirping of the birds she'd enjoyed so much yesterday now sounded as shrill as an out-of-tune violin.

Carafe in hand, she retreated to the shady privacy of the walled patio behind the casita. Beyond the wrought iron fence, she had an unimpeded view of the lake and surrounding mountains. How nice to have a private entrance to the beach, she thought, settling into the comfort of the chaise lounge. She downed two cups of coffee, and for the next couple of hours, lazily alternated between reading and dozing.

It wasn't until mid-afternoon that she awakened, refreshed and ready to face the remainder of the day. She wouldn't have thought it possible, considering the volume of food she'd consumed the night before, but suddenly she was famished. Returning to the bedroom, she slipped into her turquoise bikini and gathered her thick hair up in a large clip. Finally, she pulled on the sheer cover-up and grabbed her book, towel, and a tube of sunscreen before heading to the hotel restaurant where she consumed two glasses of ice tea and a gigantic salad filled with fresh crabmeat, mangos and slivered almonds. Satisfied and feeling good again, she strolled along the palm-fringed boardwalk to claim a spot on the crowded beach.

Stretched out on her towel in the warm sand, Rayna propped herself on one elbow to watch the scores of children playing with beach toys and frolicking in the gentle waves while their mothers chased away noisy birds swooping down on half-eaten picnic lunches. Out on the water, a sprinkling of sailboats leaned into the steady breeze. The tingle on her skin two hours later warned her that she'd had enough sun. Moving beneath the shade of a thatch-roofed ramada, she closed her eyes and fell into a deep sleep.

When she awakened sometime later, she sat up, feeling slightly disoriented. The beach was practically empty. She looked at her watch, surprised to realize that she'd slept for almost three hours. The sun had already disappeared and a full moon was rising behind the rugged peaks. Yawning, she pulled on her cover-up, picked up her belongings and strolled nonchalantly along the shoreline, allowing the warm water to lap against her bare feet, while returning the friendly greetings of the handful of bathers still remaining on the beach. Instead of using the main entrance to her casita by way of the hotel courtyard, she decided to extend her evening walk and enter through the private gate leading to her back patio.

All at once, her eyes fastened on the form of a man striding towards her, backlit by the twilight sky. There was something familiar about the set of his muscular shoulders, the narrow waist and hips, the long legs. Staring in disbelief, she stopped dead in her tracks as the figure bore down upon her. No, it couldn't *possibly* be him.

CHAPTER TEN

Her heart beating fiercely, Rayna let the towel and book slip from her limp fingers and land with a soft thud on the sand as Tyler closed the distance between them and placed himself squarely in her path. For a few seconds she stared at him in breathless amazement, unable to determine whether she was angry or ridiculously ecstatic to see him. "I don't believe it. How...how did you..." she stammered, although the moment the words left her lips, she already knew the answer. Mrs. Ansel, of course. "I mean, what are you doing here?"

"Looking for you." The voice was calm, but his face looked as hard as the volcanic peaks rimming the lake.

"Why?" she shot back with a good dose of venom in her tone.

"Why?" he repeated incredulously. "Because I have no intention of standing idly by while you pull your vanishing act on me again."

"You've got a colossal nerve breezing down here after what you did to me yesterday."

"I wouldn't exactly call what I had to go through to get here breezing," he snapped, dragging a hand through his wavy brown hair. "I had a hell of a time trying to get a flight here at the last minute."

"Well, that was your choice, I didn't ask you to come."

Tyler fought to maintain his temper. "All I ask is a fair hearing from you. You owe me that."

She strode past him. "I owe you nothing! Now please leave me alone."

"Wait!" he shouted after her, "We have to talk."

"Go away! We have nothing to discuss." Seeing the arched gate to her patio directly ahead, she quickened her pace, eager to get away, but at the same time filled with a curious excitement. No. She must not allow her treacherous heart to betray her again. She pushed through the gate, rushed across the patio and threw open the sliding door just as Tyler intercepted her.

"Oh, no, you don't," he growled, breathing heavily. He caught her by the shoulder and whirled her around to face him. "You're not running out on me this time."

"Let go of me!" she cried, struggling free. Furious tears leapt to her eyes as she fought to suppress the spontaneous rush of desire his touch evoked.

"Rayna, I'm serious. If I have to tie you up and gag you, you're going to listen to what I have to say!"

Her stomach fluttered as his eyes raked hungrily over her body. Instinctively, she clutched the flimsy cover-up to her chest. "Why are you doing this to me?" she choked, her voice rising an octave. "Deliberately forcing your way back into my life...pretending that you care...."

"Pretending?" he cut in harshly. "Is that what you think?"

"That's exactly what I think. And," she added, building up a full head of steam, "if you hadn't been in such a hurry to bump me off the case, you could have saved yourself the time and trouble since I'd already decided to step aside. So all that backdoor maneuvering with the photos...." Her voice faltering, she bit her lip to stem the tears threatening to flow.

His intense gaze darkened. "I didn't show Freestone the pictures," he said through gritted teeth. "Scott did."

"Oh, right. And where did *he* get them?"

"The prints came back while I was out of town. The concierge gave them to Scott."

Trembling with emotion, she eyed him skeptically. "Why should I believe you?"

He let out a frustrated groan. "Because it's the truth, damn it!"

Before she could protest, he reached for her again and brought his lips down to hers, kissing her with such force that it sent the tortoise-shell comb holding her hair in place clattering to the floor. She gasped as his other hand brushed the curve of her breast, then tightened around her waist. His touch ignited a bonfire within her even as she tried to push him away.

Her resistance heightened Tyler's growing excitement. The intoxicating taste of her lips, the subtle, fresh scent of her hair—silky black between his fingers— and the feel of her bare flesh, accelerated the mad beating of his heart. He pulled away long enough to whisper in her ear, "Oh, Rayna, you don't know how much I've missed you," before capturing her lips once more.

Her head spun with confusion. She should stop. Now. Before it was too late. But as his kiss deepened, she felt her resistance crumbling.

As her lips gradually parted in acquiescence, he gripped her tighter, molding her against him, delighting in the sensation of her soft breasts.

Rayna was breathless when he finally released her, astounded by the immense inner force compelling her to throw aside her reservations. It wasn't too late, she reminded herself. She could still remove herself from this alarming temptation. In spite of his forceful embrace, she was certain he would respect her wishes if she truly wanted him to stop. But even as she agonized over it, she made no effort to keep her cover-up from sliding to the ground, or to object when he lifted her into his arms and carried her inside to the bedroom.

Her thick, loose hair cascading over his arm, Tyler lowered her onto the bed and stood looking down at her, drinking in the smooth curves of her body highlighted by the bright moonlight streaming in the open window. "I want to see all of you," he murmured, reaching to unhook the front closure of her bikini top.

Rayna instinctively grabbed his hand to stop him. "Tyler, no. This is a mistake."

Edging closer, he searched her face. "How can that be if we both want each other?"

She couldn't stop the tremor in her voice. "Because we'll only hurt each other all over again."

"I would never intentionally hurt you."

She leveled him a solemn stare. "How do I know that, Tyler?"

"Because I love you," he murmured huskily. "Because I've always loved you."

Tears sprang to her eyes as he uttered the words— words she'd been waiting a lifetime to hear again. She took a long breath and exhaled it slowly, allowing the tension to seep from her body. "Tyler...I...."

"Shhhh. Don't say anything," he whispered, his mouth covering hers in a warm soft kiss.

This time she offered no resistance as he slowly peeled back the scanty material covering her breasts. Her breathing quickened when she read the desire in his dark gaze and felt the determination in his hands as he slid her bathing suit down over her hips.

She shifted her body to assist him and then sat up, reaching for the buttons on his shirt. With trembling fingers she pried them open and ran her hands over his chest. The sensuous feel of smooth skin and tight muscles electrified her.

Tyler's skin burned at the touch of her hands on his bare flesh while his eyes roamed her splendid nakedness, feasting on every curve. He marveled at her full breasts, so exquisite, so perfect, and the sleek lines of her hips and belly. He couldn't believe she was in his arms again and, for a moment, he was afraid to move, or even blink, lest she vanish as had all the visions of her he'd conjured up throughout those long, empty years.

His eyes sought hers again. Encouraged by the warm light of acquiescence reflected in their seductive violet depths, he quickly stripped off his clothing, then stretched out beside her, pulling her close. He sampled the sweetness of her lips while his hands eagerly explored the smooth contours of her firm body.

She moaned softly when he cupped her breast in his hand and began to gently knead. Her ragged breathing, conveying her growing excitement, intensified the fire consuming him. Temporarily abandoning her lips, he flicked his tongue lazily around one luscious nipple and then the other, teasing them to hard peaks.

As his fingers drifted down her flat belly to caress the satiny softness of her inner thighs, she arched against the pressure of his hand. And when she felt him delve into her warm depths, she responded in an instinctive rhythm.

His pulse shot higher as she gasped out his name, her supple body writhing against him. He could hold back no longer. Driven to the end of his endurance, he positioned himself firmly over her. "Oh, Rayna," he whispered. "I have never in my life wanted anything as much as I want you right now."

A shudder rippled through her as she felt his rigid silkiness between her thighs. It had been a long time since she'd been with a man. Her carnal need unleashed, she tugged him to her as white-hot fire raced through her veins, inciting a passion long dormant. "Yes, oh, yes," she cried out with both pain and pleasure as he laid claim to her innermost essence. She fastened her mouth on his, devouring it as though she were seeking life-giving nectar, relinquishing it only briefly to nibble on his neck before journeying back to his lips with renewed hunger. Her legs wrapped around him, she strained upwards, taking him deeper inside, matching his tempo, losing herself to the sublime sensation of flesh on flesh.

Fueled by the frenzied hunger of her lips consuming his, by her strangled screams of release, Tyler closed his eyes and gave in to the hot spasms that engulfed him, his cries mingling with hers as his passion exploded, uniting them in exquisite fulfillment.

As his breathing slowly returned to normal, he lavished slow, soft kisses on her face, her neck and her shoulders, before he gently withdrew and eased his weight to her side.

The tide of molten waves inside her subsiding, Rayna knew with absolute certainty that no matter what happened from this point on, this was a night she would cherish forever. Never would she forget a single detail of the magic that enveloped them—the moonlight spilling in the window, the breeze whispering through the palms outside, billowing the curtains and perfuming the room with the scent of honeysuckle. She had to remind herself that she wasn't dreaming. And even as nagging doubts fluttered at the edge of her mind, she pushed them away, unwilling to break the spell as she basked in the sweet elixir of love, treasuring the miracle of their having found one another once again. And the future? How could she even think of the future when she was still bowled over by the present?

As a deep silence pervaded, Rayna suspected that Tyler had fallen asleep. Edging a look at him, she was startled to find him closely observing her. She shivered with delight when he reached out a hand and slowly traced the outline of her body.

"You seemed to be in deep thought," he said, his gaze penetrating hers. "No regrets, I hope."

"Not for a second," she purred, languidly laying a hand on his hip as she slipped one leg over his.

His throat tight with emotion, Tyler whispered reverently, "Rayna, you're as beautiful as ever. More, if that's possible." He gently ran a finger over her lips. "You do believe me when I tell you that I never, ever stopped loving you?" He kissed her deeply, then gathered her to him and buried his face in her hair. When he heard no response, he raised his head, his eyes searching hers. "What's wrong?"

"I want to," she said, her voice quavering. "More than anything. But if what you say is true, then why did you marry Camille?"

A look of misery clouded his eyes. "I didn't want to marry her."

"Oh, please!" she sighed, turning away from him. "That doesn't make any sense."

"It's true." He sat up and leaned back against the headboard, drawing her up beside him. "There's a lot you don't understand. It's driven me nearly insane knowing that you thought I betrayed you, knowing how much I must have hurt you. But I had no choice. It was the only thing I could do to protect you and your family."

A chill swept over her. "What on earth are you talking about?"

He closed his eyes and rested his forehead in one hand. "I've gone over it a thousand times in my mind and now that I finally have the opportunity to tell you, I'm afraid I'll sound like a babbling idiot."

"Slow down and start at the beginning," she urged, reaching out to stroke his face.

He kissed the palm of her hand and took a measured breath before meeting her eyes again. "I'd been dating Camille on and off for about a year when I met you. Her father and mine did business together and our families belonged to the same country club. She was a girl who was...."

"More socially acceptable than me. More acceptable than the poor little girl whose parents were lowly peons working at your father's plant." She was sorry as soon as she said it, not meaning to sound so bitter.

He looked chastened. "You and I both knew my father was dead set against me marrying you. But I was young, I was stupid and I thought I could make him change his mind." He tightened his jaw. "That night after I left you...he was waiting for me at home. He raised holy hell and warned me that if I tried to see you again, he would ruin your family."

She stared at him in disbelief. "What are you talking about?"

"He told me that he would arrange things to look as though your father had been embezzling money from the company."

Rayna bristled. "What? And just how did he plan to do that without evidence? My father was the most honest man in the world!"

He gave her a cynical look. "Your father was one employee among a stable of other bookkeepers. Do you think a powerful man like my father would really have much trouble manufacturing the proof he would need to carry out such a threat? Just the charge itself would have been enough to tarnish your father's reputation, not to mention the legal quagmire it would have created. You of all people can understand that."

"Would he really have done that?" she asked hoarsely, feeling the heat rise in her face.

"I don't know. The fact is that I believed he would, and I loved you too much to let that happen. He knew how vital the medical insurance was for your little brother. It would have been devastating if your parents had lost their jobs. And with his influence in Summersville, he could have prevented them from finding jobs anywhere in the state."

Stunned, Rayna fell silent as the full impact of Tyler's revelation sank in. While she had spent a lifetime misjudging him, he had made the supreme sacrifice on her behalf. And in return she'd closed her heart to him and fled, leaving everything that mattered behind in Summersville. She cleared her throat. "But, what about your engagement announcement that appeared in the newspaper the very next day?"

"Nobody was more surprised than I was," he said with a resigned shrug. "I wish...I wish I'd had the courage to stand up to my father, to tell him flat out that I would run away and take you with me...but, what could I do? I was twenty, I had no money of my own, no job, no formal education, and most damning of all, there was still the threat against your family. I felt trapped." He took her face in his hands, a look of profound regret clouding his eyes. "When I found out you'd married someone else and left town the following week...." His voice faltered. "My life would have been bearable if I'd at least been able to hold onto the hope that you still loved me."

The tears she'd been holding back blurred her vision and spilled down her cheeks. "You know I loved you, but I didn't think you loved me! I had to go away."

"Why?"

"No one would make a big deal of it nowadays, but that was then. It was a small town and my parents were very strict. I was afraid...afraid to shame them. Oh, Tyler," she sobbed, "I was carrying your baby!"

His face was a mask of horrified shock. "Jesus, Rayna, why didn't you tell me?"

"What could you have done?"

"I don't know...something." His voice assumed a note of wonder. "We have a child?"

She looked away, crestfallen. "No. The baby was stillborn." Consumed by the never-ending grief, her voice shook. "I held him in my arms for hours, praying that a miracle would happen, that somehow he would start breathing...Tyler, he was so beautiful. He had your face, your hair...."

"Oh, Rayna, my darling, I'm sorry. So sorry," he choked, pulling her into his embrace and stroking her hair.

Overwhelmed by the intense confluence of emotions, she surrendered to the safe haven of his arms, finally able to release the sorrow that had held her heart captive. The tears flowed freely—cleansing tears, tears of relief now that she had finally shared her excruciating burden with him, now that the weight of her painful secret had at last been lifted. With every last vestige of misunderstanding swept away, the remaining traces of resentment she'd harbored against him vanished.

Hearing her heartrending sobs, Tyler closed his eyes, unable to contain his own tears of grief—for her, for himself, the infant son he had lost, for the time they had both so foolishly wasted. He held her until her weeping subsided and then he showered her face with kisses— sweet, tender kisses. She returned them and little by little, as his fingers coasted along her skin, she felt a rekindling of desire.

As they surrendered to their passion for one another, as their bodies once again blended into one, sharing the same fulfillment, the same fiery release, Rayna experienced something beyond the all-consuming physical union, beyond the enraptured journey of rediscovery. Deep in her heart now dwelt total trust and...forgiveness.

Later, snuggled in his arms and blissfully spent, Rayna drifted into a tranquil sleep until Tyler's gentle touch on her cheek wakened her. She opened her eyes and saw him propped on an elbow beside her in the near-darkness.

"What time is it?" she asked, stretching languidly with a yawn.

"Almost midnight," he said, grinning. "Long past time for dinner."

"You shouldn't have let me sleep so long," she scolded lightly, sitting up in bed.

"If I hadn't found looking at you so enjoyable," he said, allowing his appreciative gaze to travel over her once more, "I would have done the same thing myself."

She beamed with pleasure and briefly touched her lips to his. "The poets say you can live on love alone," she said in a throaty murmur, "but in your case I think you deserve some sustenance."

"You and me both."

"We're too late for the restaurant. I think it closes at ten."

"Don't tell me that's the only place in town to eat?"

"I think there may be one or two little taverns still open in the village."

"Great, let's go." He switched on the bedside lamp and reached for his jeans, pulling them on as he rose. Noticing his wallet had fallen onto the tile floor, he picked it up and looked inside, his mouth falling open in surprise. "Uh-oh. I never had time to go the bank. I don't have anything but credit cards. Do you think that will be a problem?"

"Maybe. They're just *cervecerias,* little local bars that serve food."

"Well then, it appears we may have a bit of a problem...unless you can spring for dinner," he added, with a devilish grin.

"Sure, I'll spring for dinner." She rose and stood close to him, running one finger slowly down the center of his bare chest. "And you'll have all night to pay me back."

SYLVIA NOBEL

CHAPTER ELEVEN

Ten minutes after the plane roared off the runway of the sleepy little airport and gained altitude, Rayna stared pensively out the window as a smattering of white clouds cast their shadows over the landscape, slowly obscuring the last traces of Lake Bonita reflecting the soft pastel pink glow of the setting sun. How she hated to see the precious twenty-four hours she'd just spent with Tyler come to an end. Though minuscule in the span of a lifetime, they had been among the most memorable of her life. Would she ever again experience anything so perfect, feel so totally loved, so unreservedly desired? She turned towards Tyler, not surprised to find him already dozing beside her.

Leaning back in her seat, she closed her eyes and smiled to herself as scenes from the previous night replayed in her mind. Their passion for each other had been insatiable and she'd have been surprised if either of them had slept a total of four hours. Yet they were up early, welcoming the dawn, anxious to maximize the time they had left. After sharing a cozy breakfast of fruit and warm muffins, they'd embarked on a free-spirited exploration of the lake, laughing, kissing and talking endlessly as they strolled barefoot along the beach hand in hand.

After wandering for hours, they had happened upon a small tavern perched on the edge of a cliff. In spite of the dilapidated wood-plank floor, ragged vinyl tablecloths and mismatched metal chairs, the place exuded a certain old world charm. And because it was too early for the customary lunch hour, the place became a private haven for just the two of them.

Selecting a shady table with an unimpeded view of the lake below, they enjoyed the fragrant scent of exotic flowers blooming all around them. Soon they were sipping cold papaya juice as they watched a white-haired woman with a leathery brown face pat balls of dough between her palms, stretch them into wafer-thin tortillas, then place them on the top of an ancient wood stove.

While the tantalizing, smoky aroma emanating from the kitchen promised that the grilled chicken they'd ordered would be delicious, a plate of ceviche took the edge off their hunger. The shrimp, marinated in lime juice and chilies, was exquisite and delectable wrapped in the fresh, hot tortillas. It was a challenge trying to master the art of eating the local delicacy without letting the peppery juices trickle down their wrists onto their T-shirts and jeans.

After lunch, they'd hiked back to the hotel and spent the remainder of the afternoon cuddling on the beach, never out of each other's reach, savoring every moment as if it were their last before making their way to the airport for the return flight to Tucson.

As Tyler now shifted in his sleep, Rayna studied his handsome, sculptured profile. He seemed at peace, as though he hadn't a care in the world. Unburdening themselves to each other had instilled a sense of spiritual healing as they shared feelings and experiences neither had confided to anyone else. At first he'd been reluctant, but had finally opened up to her, chronicling his joyless marriage to Camille. He'd tried to convince himself that he could make it work, but after Scott's birth, he'd begun to withdraw more and more. Sadly, he'd acknowledged that his distant demeanor had probably contributed to her descent into alcohol and drug abuse. He'd wanted to dissolve the union, but had decided, for Scott's sake, that he would remain married until his son's graduation from high school. In retrospect, he admitted that his decision had probably added to the alienation between him and Scott. In turn, Rayna clarified how she'd come to marry her childhood friend Thomas Manchester, whose family lived next door to her aunt in the small town of Whitton, where she'd fled after discovering her pregnancy.

Remembering her brief marriage brought a melancholy smile to her lips. Dear, sweet Thomas. He'd offered her love and marriage, even though he knew she carried another man's child. And when he'd accepted the offer of a larger grocery chain to relocate first to Oklahoma City and then Tucson, Rayna knew he'd made the move solely for her sake. He had been too attached to his close-knit family to leave his hometown under any other circumstance.

After the tragedy of the baby's death, she'd made a valiant effort to make the marriage work, but her heart remained numb. Sensing her need for distance, he'd consented to separate bedrooms and gradually their relationship had evolved into that of good friends rather than husband and wife. He had never complained about the arrangement. She had earned her GED and was in her third year of college when Thomas had been diagnosed with inoperable brain cancer. She had cared for him until his death, and even though she had never loved him in the same way he had loved her, she regarded him so highly that she'd made the decision to retain his name when she began practicing law. She owed him that much.

Rayna sighed deeply, happy to finally be able to put the past behind her. Right now there was nothing in the world she wanted more than to be with Tyler—yet there were still obstacles ahead: the stress of his son's trial, the fact that he was still legally married, and the daunting prospect she'd pushed to the back of her mind that suddenly rose to the forefront. What of her career, the years of study, the personal struggle to achieve her present professional status? Was she willing to sacrifice all that and consider returning to South Carolina to be with him?

The flight attendant's sudden announcement that they were on approach to Tucson International Airport jolted Tyler from his sleep. He looked around, surprised, as if he'd forgotten where he was.

"Did you have a peaceful nap?" she asked tenderly, buckling her seat belt. "You certainly earned it."

His smile appeared strained and there was a haunted faraway look in his dark eyes. "Thanks."

During the silence that followed, Rayna sensed his distress. "Tyler, is there something wrong?"

"No."

"Are you sure?"

He ran a hand across his brow. "I just had a disturbing dream, that's all."

"Not about us, I hope," she said, anxiously searching his eyes for signs of regret.

"No, no, " he said, enfolding her hand in his and squeezing it tightly. "It was about Scott. I'm just sick about this whole situation."

Rayna hoped her smile was comforting. "That's not an unnatural emotion considering...."

"Considering what happened. And that's what is bothering me. There's something very odd about this whole scenario, but I can't put my finger on it."

"What do you mean?" She felt perfectly relaxed discussing Scott's dilemma now that she was no longer involved with the case.

"Well, for starters, ever since I've been here, he seems like a different person. I mean...he's never been terribly communicative, but the way he's been acting towards me is...well, out of character."

"Most teens are uncommunicative," Rayna said with a sympathetic smile.

Tyler shook his head. "No, it's more than that. He's hiding something."

Rayna's interest perked up. "What do you mean?"

"He's always vague about where he's going when he leaves the hotel. I mean, how many friends could he have? He's only been in Tucson a few weeks."

"What's he doing here anyway?"

Tyler stared at her, puzzled. "I wish I knew. He'd been away at school and seemed to be doing well in his studies. Right after Christmas he told us he was going to Birmingham with his roommate and another friend to visit this boy's family. The next thing I know I'm getting a call from him and he's in jail in Tucson."

"He didn't come here with his classmates?"

"No, they're back in school."

They both sat silent, lost in thought. Finally Rayna asked, "Where does he work?"

"At a place called Barnaby's."

"That's a nice place. I've eaten there. So...he must be hanging out with people from work."

"Probably," Tyler responded thoughtfully. "Maybe that's where he met her."

"Met who?" Rayna asked.

"I don't know. A girl called the room and when I answered she hung up. It's happened a couple of times."

"So, he's got a girlfriend?"

"Apparently. But get this, when I questioned him regarding that subject, he denied it. There have been quite a few times that I didn't hear him come in until the early hours of the morning, and more than once, he's spent the night somewhere else." Raking a hand through his hair, he blew out a despondent sigh. "I can't prove it, but I know he was with somebody at the hotel while I was gone last week." He filled her in on his suspicions, citing the nearly empty eye shadow container in the waste can and his missing watch.

Rayna digested all the information before inquiring, "Can you think of any reason Scott would take your watch? Do you think he pawned it?"

Tyler's face fell. "I honestly don't know. I know you're going to think I'm making excuses for him because he's my son, but there is something else that's bugging me far more than that."

"What?"

He looked at her expectantly. "Do you remember during the witness's testimony when she said in her opinion, the driver was probably drunk because the SUV was weaving all over the place?"

"Yes."

"Scott doesn't drink."

Rayna's eyes widened with surprise. "Really? Not at all?"

"Nope. Not unless he's taken up drinking in the last couple of weeks."

Rayna hesitated telling him what was on her mind, but then decided it might be best. "Tyler, half of the DUI

135

cases we prosecute don't involve alcohol. I don't mean to worry you, but have you considered the possibility that he may be using drugs? You'd be amazed how many young people are driving around high as a kite on crystal meth or any other number of controlled substances."

Tyler pressed his lips together. "I find that hard to believe. This kid is...was a straight arrow. We had our disagreements, but even with the constant turmoil in our household, he always seemed to have a good head on his shoulders, and believe me, it's because of his mother's situation that he's experienced firsthand how drugs and alcohol can screw up your life." He paused, his eyes filled with torment. "You must have handled a lot of cases like this, or at least similar. What do you make of it?"

Rayna shook her head slowly. "I don't know. Something doesn't add up." She paused for a second before suggesting, "You may want to talk to Freestone about hiring a private investigator."

"Freestone," he growled, his eyes hardening with anger. "Because of his unscrupulous maneuvering...going behind my back after you, I ought to fire him."

Rayna laid a finger against his lips to silence him. "Don't do that. And don't think I don't appreciate the sentiment, I really do. It's just that while I may not agree with some of his tactics, he's still the best defense attorney in Tucson. You owe it to Scott to have him on your side."

Tyler's gaze softened. "Okay, I'll call him when he gets back on Thursday," he said, reaching out to gently stroke her cheek with the back of his hand. "Now, what do you say we not talk about this anymore. I want to talk about us and I want to thank you for giving me such a wonderful gift."

She raised a quizzical brow. "And what gift might that be?"

"A blue sky day," he said, a whimsical smile touching his lips. "I never thought I'd ever experience that feeling again after you left Summersville."

"Oh, Tyler," she whispered, her throat tightening with emotion. "Me neither."

"Right now, all I want is to see you tomorrow and the day after and the day after that for as long as I'm here."

His ardent words filled her heart with joy. "I'm counting on it," she said with a slight catch in her voice.

His dark eyes full of purpose, Tyler leaned in closer, capturing her lips in a tender kiss that might have gone on forever but for the sudden jolt of the plane's wheels meeting the runway. Pulling back reluctantly, he sighed, his eyes never leaving hers. "Can you take the day off tomorrow? I have got to get out of that hotel room and do something or I'm going to go nuts. I've been studying the Arizona map," he said, his face lighting up with enthusiasm. "What do you say we just get in the car and drive someplace for a picnic? And while we're at it, I can try out my new camera and lenses on some of the fantastic scenery around here."

Her face clouded with disappointment. "Oh, I wish I could, but, my schedule is pretty heavy tomorrow. I'll be tied up until at least five o'clock."

"I understand," he said, giving her hand a reassuring squeeze. "Well then, how about meeting me at the hotel when you've finished for the day and we'll go someplace nice for dinner? You choose."

His proposal resurrected her spirits. "What time?"

"Whenever works best with your schedule. I'll plan on getting back to the hotel around three or four at the latest." His eyes held a suggestive glint. "Come by any time after that. Perhaps a little afternoon siesta will be in order by then. Would you care to join me?"

The surge of pleasurable anticipation warmed her cheeks. "Sounds like a plan."

***

Monday morning, as she'd expected, Rayna was besieged by members of the news media, all shoving microphones in her face and demanding an explanation for her sudden withdrawal from the high-profile case. Maintaining a cool, professional demeanor, she parsed her words and finally escaped the barrage of questions. Relieved that the challenging ordeal was behind her, at least for the time being, she blew out a sigh of relief and hurried inside the court complex, her thoughts immediately turning to Tyler. She tingled with pleasure as she relived his long passionate kiss goodnight the previous evening. He'd been gone only a few moments when Mrs. Ansel arrived at her door to return Beauregarde. In the middle of her profuse apology for revealing Rayna's whereabouts to Tyler, the older woman appeared bewildered when, instead of receiving a reprimand, she'd received an enthusiastic hug. And it was obvious to Rayna when she'd checked her phone messages later that Mrs. Ansel had also spilled the beans to Tracy, who had left three messages chastising her for her secrecy and demanding that she be called immediately upon her return.

Her lips curved in a confident smile, Rayna entered her law offices eager to bring Miguel up to date on the strange and wonderful turn the weekend had taken. She owed him a huge debt of thanks for his suggestion that she spend the weekend in Mexico. Looking back, she could hardly believe it herself. To her surprise, she learned from the receptionist that his wife, Angelina, had given birth to a little girl a few hours earlier. When she checked her voicemail messages there was one from Miguel assuring her that everything was fine and that he would be off work for a few days. No doubt they'd have their hands full now with four children. She scratched out a reminder in her day planner to buy a baby gift at the mall.

Humming a happy little tune, she threw herself wholeheartedly into the work that had accumulated since Friday morning, tackling it without even a break for lunch, hoping to get as much accomplished as she could before her afternoon hearing. When she was later notified that the preliminary hearing had been postponed until the following week, she regretted that she hadn't been able to accept Tyler's invitation to join him on his outing.

But the unexpected time gave her an opportunity to take another look at the Brockwell file before Mitchell reassigned it to one of her colleagues. As she carefully poured over the police report and the witness's testimony once again, the sinking feeling in her stomach grew more intense. If Scott had been under the influence of alcohol or drugs, that would provide an explanation for his reckless behavior. But if he had been sober as Tyler suggested, his heartless demeanor following the accident painted the story of a very different person altogether. She tapped her fingers on the desk and absently stared out the window at the construction workers repairing a rooftop across the street. Tyler's description of his son's conduct prior to the accident added a new and puzzling dimension to the case.

Thinking back to the preliminary hearing, something lurked at the edge of her memory. But as hard as she tried, she could not recall what it was. While she could only imagine the pain of being a parent in this situation, it was enough to set a chain of thoughts in motion. Suddenly filled with restless energy, the germ of an idea began to take shape in her mind. She'd read hundreds of reports and worked with police and sheriff's detectives for many years. Perhaps there was something she could do to help ease Tyler's torment until Freestone's return. With no clear purpose in mind, she left word that she would be out the rest of the afternoon.

Twenty minutes later Rayna drove into the parking lot of Barnaby's, the upscale restaurant where Scott Brockwell worked. It was almost two o'clock. She'd patronized the restaurant many times in the past, and knew that it closed after lunch and re-opened for dinner at five. It was a long shot that he would be working this shift, but a tingle of triumph rippled through her when she noticed his SUV parked at the far end of the lot. She pulled into a shady spot and waited. Fifteen minutes later, her pulse rate picked up when Scott ambled out the door, loped across the parking lot and climbed into his vehicle.

"It's show time," she whispered to herself, starting the engine. Still questioning the sanity of her actions, Rayna followed him to an old residential neighborhood that had seen better days. She took note of the fact that the vehicle Scott was driving had Alabama plates. Had that been in the police report? She slowed when his brake lights came on, and watched him turn left into a driveway and accelerate past a rundown two-story house, complete with peeling green paint and a sagging porch. A mangy-looking dog chained to a tree in the front yard, barked at her. She cruised by the mouth of the driveway long enough to see him stop in front of what appeared to be a small guest cottage to the rear of the main house. He jumped out and the front door swung open. The interior of the house was too dark for Rayna to make out the identity of the person who reached out a hand and pulled him inside. The door closed immediately.

Rayna's curiosity kicked into high gear as she parked her car across the street. How odd. Scott Brockwell had grown up in a household where money was no object. He'd probably never lacked for anything, at least of material value. So, why would he choose to live in such a ramshackle place in one of the poorer neighborhoods in Tucson? And if this was where he stayed when he wasn't with Tyler at the hotel, why the secrecy? She drummed on the steering wheel, trying to decide what, if anything, she should do next. She couldn't very well present herself at the door demanding information. Scott would surely recognize her.

For a fleeting moment she entertained the idea of just returning to the office, but the compelling desire to find out if Tyler's suspicions held water overruled her hesitation. She waited another ten minutes to see if he would reappear, and when he didn't, she put the car in gear and circled the block several times, her mind working to formulate some plan of action. After the third time around, she stopped suddenly when a sanitation truck pulled out in front of her and trundled down the street. She turned and stared into a weed-strewn alleyway. If she was correct, it ran directly behind the cottage. She eased to the curb, got out and locked the car behind her. After a quick look around, she slipped into the oleander-fringed alley. The loose gravel crunching beneath her shoes set off a chorus of barking dogs from several homes nearby. Still unsure as to what she planned to do, she stood on tiptoe and looked over the block wall until she recognized the green house. Cautiously, she approached the wooden gate, lifted the latch, and peeked through the opening. Good. The casement windows on the cottage were all open. But then her heart sank. In order to reach the guesthouse she would have to navigate thirty or forty feet of open space before reaching the shelter of the junipers and rose bushes bordering it. She'd be in full view if anyone were watching from the main house. She drew back, her logical mind rebelling. This was crazy. Why risk getting caught trespassing in someone's yard? Worse yet, what if Scott and whoever else was inside the cottage caught her eavesdropping? She turned and started to walk back towards her car, but then her footsteps slowed. No. If she could do something, anything, to allay Tyler's anguish, wasn't it worth a try? Before she could change her mind a second time, she returned to the gate and pushed it open. Gathering her courage, she sprinted across the yard, all the while fighting the desire to laugh hysterically. She ducked behind the bushes, her heart pumping wildly. What was she thinking, skulking around like someone in a Nancy Drew mystery novel? If she were going to play detective, at least she should have dressed more suitably for the part, she thought, ruefully wishing she'd worn slacks instead of the short navy skirt. Her only consolation was that at least she'd worn a pair of low-heeled shoes.

On hands and knees, she crept up to the window and crouched below it, wincing in silence as she plucked several rose thorns from her fingers. Cautiously, she raised her head and peeked through the grimy screen into a small room, simply furnished with a loveseat faced away from her, two chairs and a coffee table piled with magazines, cups and empty Styrofoam food containers. A TV in the corner was tuned in to a popular daytime soap opera. Her eyes were drawn to a pair of bare feet sporting bright pink nail polish, dangling over one end of the loveseat, not two feet from where she crouched in the dirt.

She flinched when Scott suddenly entered the room but, seconds before ducking out of sight, she caught a glimpse of him brandishing a bottle, his expression livid. Keeping her breathing shallow, she knelt below the windowsill, listening to the obvious agitation in his voice. "I guess you didn't have time to get rid of the evidence today."

"What are you talking about?" came a bored reply, accompanied by a big yawn.

"Right, like you don't know where this came from."

"Oh, come on," the female voice countered, "so I have a beer once in a while. It's not going to hurt me this early."

"Damn it, Aubrey! You promised me you'd lay off the booze."

"Baby, don't get mad over one little ol' beer," she cajoled huskily. "It's not the end of the world."

"The hell it isn't! Your stupid drinking has made a mess of everything. Jesus, weren't you listening when I told you what Freestone said? They're going to send my ass to jail! I'm starting to think you don't really care what happens to me."

"Of course I do, sweetie pie," the girl insisted, patiently. "Now, did you ask your father for the money like we talked about?"

"Not yet," he mumbled.

"What are you waiting for? My uncle isn't going to let us stay here free forever."

Following a short silence, Rayna heard Scott say, "He's gonna know something's up if I ask him for a grand. He's not stupid. I'm the one who's stupid for going along with this in the first place."

"Don't freak out on me now. You agreed that this was the best thing to do. It's going to be okay, really."

"None of this is turning out okay." His voice choked. "I hate it! I've got to tell my dad what really...."

"No! No! You can't do that, Scottie. You know what will happen if they find out about me being in trouble before."

Rayna picked up the shrill note of panic underscoring the girl's words and heard her feet hit the floor. "Are you forgetting about the baby?"

"Am I forgetting? That's what this whole frickin' nightmare is all about, isn't it?"

Rayna stifled a gasp. She was learning far more than she had bargained for.

"If you really cared about the baby you wouldn't be drinking at all," he groused. "Where'd you get the money to buy this booze, huh? Did you take my dad's watch?"

"Stop preaching," she cooed. "I promise I'll stop drinking. I really will this time. Let's not fight anymore. Come here, big guy, I'll make you feel better."

The ensuing silence prompted Rayna to hazard another look inside. She'd been crouching in the same position for so long, her knees cracked as she edged upward. She held her breath, horrified that they may have heard it, but when nothing happened she peeked inside again. Scott and Aubrey were wrapped in each other's arms, apparently oblivious to anything else.

Rayna stared at them for a few seconds before the realization set in. Holy cow! They could pass for twins.

Long legs clad in identical stonewashed jeans, loose, pale-blonde shoulder-length hair—the witness's testimony flashed through her mind. Given the dim light and only a fleeting glimpse of the fast-moving vehicle, she could understand how one would be hard-pressed to distinguish between the two.

As they drew apart, Rayna got a clear view of the girl's face. The delicate features, the sultry brown eyes... Wait a minute. Was this the same girl Scott had been silently communicating with at the preliminary hearing, the one with the big straw hat? Everything began to fall into place—Scott's lack of remorse, his secretive behavior and the mysterious phone calls. She had a strong suspicion that it had been Aubrey, not Scott, driving the SUV that night. And if the girl had priors on her record—that, and her present condition, provided more than enough motivation for his decision to shoulder the blame for the accident. All she had to do now was prove it. Burning to share her news with Tyler, she turned to slip away, but in her haste, she stumbled over a root. Instinctively, she reached out to steady herself and bumped against the wooden siding of the house.

"What was that?" Scott asked, his voice fearful.

Rayna dropped to the ground, her heart slamming painfully against her ribs, the fear of discovery making her lightheaded when she heard movement at the window. He must have been standing directly above her head because she could hear his rapid breathing

"It's probably the neighbor's cat again," she heard Aubrey call out impatiently. "Come on back, baby. Let's have some fun."

Rayna exhaled a long, silent breath of relief when she heard Scott move away from the window. She waited another minute or so, then crawled out from behind the bushes and dashed across the yard. When she reached her car, she slumped weakly behind the wheel and waited for her frazzled nerves to calm. Wow. She'd never done anything so bold in her entire life. Ruefully, she had to admit that playing private investigator had been a real adrenaline high.

The additional and surprising information she'd gathered made an already abysmal situation even more complicated, and it weighed heavily on her mind. A glance at the clock confirmed that Tyler should be en route to his hotel by now. She dialed his cell number and was surprised when she reached his voice mail. Odd. Just as well, she decided, punching the off button. This news was too important to divulge on the phone. She started the engine and headed for the hotel, anxious to share her discovery with him in person.

CHAPTER TWELVE

It was all Rayna could do to stay at the speed limit as she made her way across town. The more she thought about it, the more she wondered if she was going to be the bearer of good news or bad? Her suspicion that Scott had not been the driver that night would be well received, but how do you tell the man you love that his first grandchild might be born in prison?

By the time she reached the hotel parking lot, the evening sky was a blazing tapestry of crimson, gold and purple. Normally, she would have taken a few minutes to enjoy the breathtaking splendor, but instead she ran into the hotel and raced into the open elevator, punching the button for the eighth floor. On the way up, she double-checked her day planner to verify his room number.

She knocked and waited. When there was no answer, she knocked again. Perhaps he hadn't returned from his outing yet. She tried his cell number but again, it went directly to voice mail. She thought briefly about ringing the room, but that seemed silly. If he were there, he would answer the door.

All at once, a pang of distress shot through her. What if he'd gotten lost? She wasn't even sure where he'd gone. And it was very possible he was in an isolated area without cell service. Unsure what to do, she nervously shifted from one foot to the other, finally deciding to leave a message at the desk for him. She turned to leave, but stopped when she heard voices coming from behind the door. Leaning closer, she listened for a few seconds before

147

discerning that it was the TV. Puzzled, she knocked again, louder this time. She knew Scott wasn't there, so why wasn't Tyler responding? Suddenly the door swung open to reveal a stunning blue-eyed blonde wrapped in a bright red silk robe. "Oh, I'm so sorry," Rayna said, feeling foolish. "I must have the wrong room."

"Who are you looking for?" the woman asked in a low, husky voice.

"Um...Tyler Brockwell."

"You have the right room."

Rayna stood speechless, her mind refusing to believe her eyes.

"I'm Camille Brockwell," the woman announced, raising one perfectly waxed brow. "And you are?"

"Rayna Manchester," she murmured, straining to hide her shock. "I...I'm from the DA's office. I...uh...had an appointment with him this afternoon."

"My son informed me earlier that he's due to be here any time now. Please come in," she said with a regal wave of one hand.

Rayna hesitated in the doorway. This was insane. What on earth would she say to Tyler's soon to be ex-wife? Her better judgment urged her to beat a hasty retreat, but the need to know why the woman was here in Tyler's hotel room, dressed in nothing other than a downright slinky-looking robe, compelled her to accept the invitation. After all, this was the woman who had shared half of Tyler's life. That thought spawned a myriad of emotions that ran the gamut from strong resentment to something akin to jealousy. Camille was far more attractive than she had expected from Tyler's description of a woman suffering from acute alcoholism.

"I take it your visit has to do with my son?" Camille inquired, closing the door to the hallway.

"In a manner of speaking," Rayna replied, side-stepping the three matching designer suitcases before seating herself on one of the plush chairs. How bizarre that her very first visit to Tyler's hotel suite would result in her meeting his estranged wife. It was understandable that she would have to come to Tucson to visit Scott, but it didn't explain why she was in Tyler's hotel room in a state of semi-undress. Camille eased onto the couch opposite her and crossed her long, well-tanned legs. "I just flew in this morning. I'd appreciate being filled in on everything that's happened in regards to Scott's situation."

Rayna shifted uncomfortably. The realization that she was there under false pretenses made the room suddenly feel airless. "I'd rather wait and speak with both of you at the same time."

"All right." She paused. The blue eyes were now scrutinizing her carefully. "I've never been to Tucson before, but for some reason you look familiar to me. What did you say your name was again?"

"Rayna Manchester."

"Rayna. That's an unusual name."

"So I've been told."

"It wouldn't happen to have a Southern origin, would it?"

The unmistakable undertone of contempt in Camille's voice, in conjunction with the woman's cool stare of appraisal, puzzled Rayna. Her instincts warned her to proceed cautiously. "I suppose it might." Was it her imagination, or was Camille playing a game of cat and mouse with her? "Are you planning to stay on until the trial?" Rayna added quickly, hoping to shift the spotlight away from herself.

"Oh, yes, indeed." A guileless look replaced the disquieting, intense expression. "My place is here with my son and my husband."

The possessive declaration made Rayna feel as though her heart had been plucked from her chest. "We were given to understand that you and Mr. Brockwell had separated."

Camille's perfectly shaped lips parted in a dazzling smile. "Well, then, you were mistaken. We are technically separated but Tyler and I have been discussing a reconciliation for several months now."

Her mouth dry as cotton, Rayna clenched her hands together. Nothing could have prepared her for such a shock. All she could think of was getting away as fast as possible. "I have to go," she said, rising abruptly.

"Oh, that's too bad. Is there a message I can give Tyler?" Camille asked, her smile polite, yet her eyes as cold as ice.

"No, I'll be in touch later." Somehow she willed her unsteady legs to transport her to the door, along the corridor, down the elevator and to her car. She tried hard to keep her wits about her in the relentless rush-hour traffic and twice almost slammed into the car ahead, her thoughts spiraling in chaos, her emotions whirling on a merry-go-round from hell. She'd risked her reputation and placed her career on the line for this man, and it required supreme effort to remain focused on traffic and not give in to the flood of tears that threatened. Fiery coals of betrayal burned her insides, along with profound feelings of devastation and shame. How could she have been so gullible? How could she have allowed herself to be used again—all in the name of love?

Her logic and emotions warred with each other. Was she doomed to be hopelessly in love with a man who claimed to love her, but who had conveniently failed to mention anything about reconciling with his wife? Had he been toying with her while keeping his options open?

Horns were now blaring around her, people shouting obscenities. "Haven't spotted a color you like, lady?" a burly truck driver was yelling down through the open window, mocking her for having overstayed her welcome at the intersection. As if in a fog, Rayna drove on, unsure as to where she was headed. She tortured herself, picturing Tyler and Camille having a cozy tête-à-tête by candlelight. There would be sincere apologies for past misbehavior, pledges of renewed love and the promise of a new life together. Stop! She couldn't bear to think of it. Why had he invited her to the hotel if he'd known that Camille would be there? Suddenly, nothing made any sense. As if operating on automatic pilot, she somehow found herself in the parking lot of the gym.

Good choice. No, great choice, she thought as she entered the brightly lit building. She was anxious to lose herself in a strenuous workout that would hopefully dull the misery engulfing her.

Inside the crowded locker room, Rayna tugged on her workout clothes, then slammed the locker shut with a bang, startling the other women. Her jaw fixed, she was determined to blank out all thoughts and physically push herself to the max until she blotted out the pain searing her insides. She almost collided with Tracy when she pushed the door open to the hallway. "Hey, there," her friend chirped with a cheery smile, "I thought you weren't coming tonight."

"My plans changed."

Reacting to her sharp tone, Tracy's smile faded. "Okay," she said slowly, trying to interpret Rayna's grim expression, "then how about keeping me company while I change? I'm dying to hear all the juicy details about your weekend trip to Mexico." She eyed Rayna with mock disdain. "Some friend you are, taking off for parts unknown in the company of your dark-eyed mystery man and not saying a word about it."

Rayna heaved a deep sigh, wishing now she hadn't even mentioned it to her when she'd returned Tracy's call earlier in the day. "Not now. First, I've got to blow off some steam."

Tracy's expression turned speculative. "When you're ready to talk, I'm all ears."

Forcing a tight smile, Rayna squeezed Tracy's shoulder and headed for the treadmill. She set it on high and pounded away the miles, focusing solely on each stride. A half hour later, drenched with perspiration, she headed for the spinning class. As she breezed by the aerobics room, Tracy stuck her head out the door. "Ready to talk now?"

"Not yet," she replied. She hurried past, ignoring her friend's bewildered expression, and entered the room, dimly lit with black lights, where the class was already in progress. She closed her eyes and pedaled hard, surrendering to the frenetic beat of the music, plunging herself once more into total concentration. An hour later, her injured morale felt somewhat restored. Yet even the catharsis of intense exercise could not prevent the afternoon's events from finally seeping back into her mind like clips from a surreal movie, beginning with her moronic sleuthing escapade. What should she do now? Considering Camille's shocking disclosure, she questioned why she should impart any of the information she'd uncovered to Tyler. Why should she lift a finger to help his son? For all she cared, Scott could rot in jail for the rest of his life.

The last thought generated an unexpected stab of guilt. Did the poor besotted kid deserve such a cruel fate? Weren't each of them suffering the same predicament? What kind of a person was she to take revenge on him just because his father was apparently disingenuous? Besides, didn't she have some sort of ethical obligation?

But even as she embraced the hurtful thoughts, something deep in her heart rejected them and began to sow the seeds of doubt. As a trained trial attorney, shouldn't she have known better than to lend credence to Camille, to blindly accept her words at face value? Was it not altogether possible that the whole notion of reconciliation was no more than wishful thinking on her part?

Rayna decreased her speed as the music slowed for recovery. She took a deep, cleansing breath while her heart rate gradually returned to normal. Was she objectively assessing the encounter with Camille, or was she having a knee-jerk emotional reaction to the woman's unsubstantiated claims? She'd been lightning-quick to judge Tyler, setting logic aside and allowing her inherent mistrust to control her. Where was her sense of fair play, of justice?

In her professional life she was the model of restraint, carefully weighing every shred of evidence, every word, every nuance. Why on earth, then, could she not apply the same principle to her personal life and grant herself the same consideration, instead of choosing to flee at the first sight of danger? It was all too clear. The problem lay with neither Camille nor Tyler. The problem, without question, lay with herself, with her lifelong pattern of distrust.

If she were to be totally honest with herself, she had to believe that Tyler Brockwell was really a truthful and decent man. If she truly loved him, then she would give him the benefit of the doubt and listen to his explanation regarding Camille's allegation. And she must be prepared to accept the consequences. Good or bad, right or wrong, she was not going to disintegrate. She would come out of this better off and stronger for having reached a final resolution with her past.

As the class wound down and the music stopped, Rayna slid off the bike and sat down on one of the benches, leaning her head back against the wall. She closed her eyes, feeling totally exhausted and yet, in a strange way, empowered.

"Planning to spend the night here, are you?"

Rayna opened her eyes and peered up into Tracy's quizzical face.

"I've just had an epiphany."

Tracy gawked at her in amazement. "Wow, I guess I'd better get myself on your workout program."

Rayna made a face at her. "I'm serious."

"So, what's the deal?" Tracy demanded. "You acted like you were going to bite my head off earlier."

Rayna smiled forlornly. "I'm sorry. I didn't mean to be so short with you. I just needed to sort some things out."

"What things?"

"It's too long and convoluted to go into now, but I promise I'll tell you everything soon."

Tracy's eyes narrowed with suspicion. "Since you're not having dinner with Tyler like you originally told me, I'm going to interpret your statement as meaning that you two have had a falling out of some kind. Would I be right?"

Rayna hesitated before answering, "We did sort of, in my head, but not actually. I mean I'm not sure it's really happened yet."

Tracy slumped down beside her. "I wish I could say I understood what you just said, but I didn't."

"Let me just put it this way. Things may not work out the way I hoped, and if they don't…well, I think I'll be okay."

"Whoa, this sounds heavy, girlfriend. I'll tell you what I think. You need to get your buns over to my place. You can spill your guts and," she added conspiratorially, "I've got my some of Mom's homemade spinach lasagna which I'm willing to share."

"Can I take a rain check?"

"On the lasagna or my offer of invaluable and totally free advice?"

"Both." Rayna threw her arms around her. "You're a good friend."

Tracy hugged her back. "Are you sure you're going to be okay?"

"Yes, I'm sure. I've got to go," she said, jumping to her feet.

"It's only nine o'clock. What's the rush?"

Rayna edged her a reflective smile. "I have to go home now and get started on the rest of my life."

CHAPTER THIRTEEN

Aware of the sudden chill, Tyler shrugged into his leather jacket and loaded the last roll of film into the Nikon camera. After carefully balancing the tripod on the rocky ground, he adjusted the shutter speed as the glorious winter sun edged towards the rugged western mountains backlit by a hazy pumpkin-colored sky. With his eye pressed against the viewfinder, he felt supremely humbled as he had all afternoon by the stark majesty of this vast arid landscape, so diametrically different from the lush green forests of home.

He doubted even the wide angle lens could begin to capture the grandeur of the wind-carved cliffs of Madera Canyon, bathed in fiery shades of coral and crimson while purple shadows slipped inside the rocky crevices in the rapidly fading light. Very few things that he'd ever experienced could match the acute sense of wonderment he felt at this moment in time.

The last shot completed, he shouldered his camera and collapsed the legs of the tripod. He hadn't meant to stay so long and, when he did consult his watch, he was stunned to realize it was already four-thirty. Damn! He was going to be late! He reached for his cell phone to let Rayna know, but to his dismay, was unable to power it on. Berating himself for not recharging the battery the previous evening as he'd planned, he quickened his pace. If he made good time, he should be able to make it back to the hotel before six o'clock. Hopefully, they'd arrive at about the same time. As he made his way along the solitary trail, he recalled each precious detail of the magical hours he'd spent with her. They'd shared so much of themselves— their desires, their hopes— as they confessed the hurts of the past, and experienced the joy of having once again found each other. Yet he recalled how quiet she'd become when he touched on the future of their relationship. Even though she tried to hide it, he sensed her reticence when he'd mentioned his eventual return to South Carolina, his gentle suggestion that perhaps she join him soon. As he loaded the equipment into the car and started down the winding dirt road towards Interstate 19, the series of random thoughts that had been lurking in his subconscious mind for the past several weeks began to come together and a rush of excitement swept over him. In a strange and tragic way, the events surrounding Scott's predicament had forced him to undergo a serious reevaluation of his own life. Didn't he have a pattern of setting aside his own dreams to please others? Hadn't he done just that when he'd caved to his father's wishes and married the woman whose family connections would most benefit the expansion of Brockwell Industries? Even though he'd longed to become a professional photographer, he'd stepped up to the plate and taken the helm after his father fell ill. And even now, five years after his father's death, with many of his competitors moving their manufacturing sites to cheaper overseas locations, he struggled to keep the business profitable because he carried a heavy weight of responsibility for the continuing welfare of his employees, many of whom were personal friends. Didn't at least half the families in Summersville depend on him?

As he merged onto Interstate 10, passing a crowded industrial area, he recognized that the time had come to chart a new course. The realization that he had the freedom to do just that sent his spirits soaring even higher. And as the downtown skyline came into view, he smiled, suddenly remembering that the gift he'd purchased for Rayna would be ready in a few days. Envisioning the look on her face when he presented it to her sent a thrill of elation through him.

Even with the delay caused by rush hour traffic, he made it to the hotel by a quarter to six. With any luck, he'd have a few minutes to freshen up before Rayna arrived. With a lively spring in his step he hurried along the corridor to his room and was relieved when he didn't see her outside his door. Good. At least she hadn't been forced to stand around waiting for him. He stuck the card in the lock, pushed the door open, and almost staggered, unable to believe his own eyes at the sight of his estranged wife lounging on the couch in front of the TV, her silky robe pulled back to expose one long leg and hanging loose around her full breasts. "Camille! What...what the hell are you doing here?" he demanded, trying not to reveal how shaken he was to see her.

Making no effort to cover herself, she pushed back her ash blonde hair, pouting prettily. "Oh, Tyler, don't be boorish. I'm here to lend moral support to Scott, of course."

Tyler focused on her suitcases. "Answer the question. What are you doing here?"

"I am still legally Mrs. Tyler Brockwell whether you like it or not." She sat up, pulling the robe tighter across her chest. "If you must know, Scott let me in. Didn't he tell you I was coming?"

Tyler glared at her. "No, he didn't, but that still doesn't explain why you're in my suite."

Her eyes brimmed with innocence. "There wasn't anything else available."

"Oh, give me a break."

"It's true. You can check for yourself. The man at the desk said there are a couple of big conventions in town and every place is booked solid. At least any place I'd want to stay," she added with a slight shrug. "And before you have a big ol' hissy fit, the manager promised he'd have a room for me tomorrow. I'm only going to be here for a couple of days and I didn't think you'd mind if I stayed here one night."

"Actually, I do mind." Tyler opened the door to Scott's room, looked inside, and then checked his own bedroom before turning to face her, arms folded.

"What are you looking for?" she asked, looking genuinely puzzled.

"Your bloodsucking attorney. Since he's been glued to your side for the past eight months while you've been busy trying to bankrupt me, I figured that he'd be here with you."

Camille's blue eyes flamed. "If you'd stop being so unreasonable and agree to my terms this could be over tomorrow," she countered frostily. "After the hell you've put me through for nineteen years, I think I'm entitled to continue living in the lifestyle I'm accustomed to."

Tyler struggled to maintain his temper. Somehow, as always, she managed to turn everything around to reflect on him. He glanced at the clock, unable to subdue a stab of panic. Rayna would be arriving any minute. How was he going to explain Camille being in his room half-dressed? And, he certainly didn't want her knowing about Rayna. That could only make an already intolerable situation worse.

"Speaking of lifestyle, you're looking well, Camille. Apparently your most recent stay in rehab has agreed with you." He knew the barb would hit home and felt a wicked thrill of satisfaction when her cheeks flamed with emotion.

"Can't we be civilized with each other for once? I came here to see if there was anything I could do to help Scott and this is the thanks I get?"

"You need not have troubled yourself. I've been on top of this thing right from the start."

"I'll just bet you have," she purred with a derisive smile.

Tyler was immediately on guard. "What's that supposed to mean?"

"Oh, nothing." The guileless look on her face belied the mockery in her voice. "I just find it so heartening to suddenly see you in the role of the dutiful father. How magnanimous of you to take time away from your precious business to rush across the country to be at your son's side in his darkest hour."

Tyler stared at her blankly. "I don't know where this is leading, but my plans for this evening don't include staying here playing word games with you." He charged towards his bedroom. "The place is all yours. I'll spend the night somewhere else."

"I have no doubt of that. Oh, and that reminds me," she added, allowing a note of sarcasm to steal into her voice, "you had a visitor earlier."

He stopped in his tracks and whirled around. "Who?"

She pinned him with an insolent glare. "Rayna Manchester."

Tyler fought keep his face expressionless even though his heart wrenched painfully. "Oh? And what did she want?"

"Not me, that's for sure." Camille rose from the couch, her eyes bright with venom. "You lying bastard. You weren't really away on business trips to Dallas or Los Angeles or wherever the hell else you claimed you had to be, were you?"

"What are you getting at?"

"You were here with her all those times, weren't you?"

Tyler's blood ran cold. "You're out of your mind."

"No, I'm not. I'm stone cold sober. It was always her, wasn't it, right from the beginning? Just please be honest for once in your life and admit it!"

"Camille, I can't do this anymore. I won't. It's too late to change anything for us...."

Her expression grew wily. "I found the picture."

Tyler rolled his eyes heavenward. "What picture?"

"Her picture! Rayna's picture!" she cried. "The one you kept hidden behind the drawer in your office all those years."

He flinched with surprise. "Oh, my God. What did you say to her?"

"Actually, we had quite a lovely chat...."

"What did you say to her?" he repeated icily.

"I told her we were planning to reconcile."

"Why?" he thundered, his fists clenched in rage, his blood pressure boiling. "Why would you tell her that?"

"Because..." she whimpered, assuming a woebegone expression. "Because, that's what I really want."

Tyler slumped into a chair, head down, his hands clenched together so hard, they felt bloodless. A long silence stretched between them, broken only by Camille's sniffling. Finally he looked up at her, saying in a quiet voice, "Camille, you have to let this go. You have to let me go."

"Oh, Tyler," she cried, dabbing her tear-stained cheeks, "don't you realize how much I loved you? All I ever wanted was for you to love me back. Please tell me you did...please tell me that you loved me...just a little."

Thrust once again into a state of familiar depression, the usual words of recrimination leaped to his throat followed by his habitual desire to flee yet another emotion-drenched quarrel. But instead, a crushing sense of remorse held him motionless, and the hurtful accusations remained unspoken. What a terrible price this woman had paid for his lack of courage. He'd condemned Camille and Scott to a life of loneliness, both of them victims of his resentful heart. On some deep level, he realized how imperative it was that whatever he said next be the right thing. "I did love you, Camille," he said softly, "and I can't apologize enough for hurting you, for causing you so much grief. I was a lousy husband and you deserved better."

Apparently weighing his words, she pressed a tissue to her nose and said nothing for a moment. Then, she gathered her composure and smiled weakly. "On that note, I'll admit I wasn't exactly a model wife either."

Tyler rose to his feet. "Good or bad, we shared a respectable number of years and had a beautiful son together. I will admit to you that I was not always a faithful husband and I'm sorry for that but," he added earnestly, "prior to two weeks ago, I swear to you that I had neither seen nor spoken to Rayna Manchester since before you and I were married. It's very important to me that you believe that."

Her eyes locked into his and she nodded slowly. "I'll try "

* * *

In a state of restless anxiety, Tyler spent the next two hours outside of Rayna's condominium, alternately sitting inside his car trying to keep warm, and pacing aimlessly in the cold night air, staring at her empty parking space while repeatedly dialing her home and cell numbers to no avail. He had even gone inside to quiz Mrs. Ansel on Rayna's whereabouts. The older woman had appeared puzzled, and Tyler could hardly blame her, since for the second time in several days he was once again at her door begging to know where Rayna was. With a sad shake of her head, she told him that she wasn't sure, although it wasn't unusual for Rayna to arrive home late some evenings. Perhaps she'd gone out to dinner with friends, Mrs. Ansel had suggested, or she may have gone to the gym. Tyler returned to his car, dismayed to note that it was fast approaching nine-thirty.

It wasn't too difficult to reach the conclusion that she was most likely avoiding him. What must she think of him with this unfortunate encounter occurring right on the heels of the episode with Freestone three days ago? He could hardly blame her if she hated him now. He envisioned her fury as he tried to explain Camille's presence in his room and her fabricated lie. If only he'd known she was coming, he could have prevented this latest debacle. But, there was no point in Monday-morning-quarterbacking.

He was debating whether to track her down at the gym or continue to wait, when all of a sudden there she was pulling into her parking space. Now that she was finally here, he hesitated. Should he confront her immediately, or approach her later inside? Instinctively, he decided against waiting and scrambled from his car shouting, "Rayna!"

At the sound of his voice, she turned sharply and watched him sprint towards her. Buoyed by her newfound confidence, her emotions no longer grounded in fear, she embraced the depths of love she felt for this man and stood ready to hear him out, regardless of the consequences.

"Hi," he panted, anxiously searching her eyes for signs of rejection, bracing for a firestorm of emotion. "I have something to tell you." He wanted to touch her in the worst way, but held back, feeling unsure of himself.

She studied his eyes and body language carefully, gratified to see no signs of discomfiture, no signs of guilt. "I thought you might."

Puzzled by her calm demeanor, he rubbed his icy hands together. "I've been waiting here calling your cell phone for more than two hours."

"I'm sorry, it was in my locker. I was at my gym working off some stress."

He eyed her with trepidation. "I can understand why you might be upset."

"I'm not upset," she interjected, keeping her voice mild. "Not anymore, at least. But, I am beat and I'm also starving since I never got that dinner you promised me."

He looked stricken. "I'm really sorry about that. Obviously, the evening didn't turn out quite as I planned."

"The evening isn't over yet," she said, unable to suppress a reflective smile. "I'm willing to listen with an open mind and I just happen to have some news to share with you, too. So, do we stand out here in the cold talking or would you rather come inside where it's warm?"

Tyler's sense of relief was so great, he felt like cartwheeling across the parking lot. "Inside would be better, but just to set the record straight, just to put your mind at ease, there isn't a grain of truth in what Camille told you about a reconciliation between us."

"Okay, but there's one thing that's really bugging me," Rayna said. "Why did I get the feeling that somehow she knew who I was?"

Tyler's face reddened. "Remember the photos I took of you that one afternoon in the daisy field?"

"Tyler Brockwell, you promised that you'd given me all the negatives."

"And I did," he replied earnestly with just a hint of sheepishness. "I just didn't tell you that I'd kept one of the prints. It was the only thing I had left of you. I thought it was safely hidden away in my study, but..."

Her heart at peace, Rayna took one of his cold hands in hers and pulled him to the doorway. "I can't fault her for wanting you back. Now, come on, I have something important to tell you."

Rayna switched on her gas fireplace and fed Beauregarde before setting out a plate of cheese and crackers for them to snack on while they waited for Chinese food to be delivered. Pressing a glass of Merlot into Tyler's hand, she sat down next to him on the couch and began to relay the results of her afternoon of sleuthing. When she shared her hypothesis with him, his expression of growing astonishment turned to triumph. "Yes!" he shouted, his eyes wide and brimming with hope. "I was right! I knew it! I knew Scott was innocent." Overwhelmed by the extraordinary news, he set his glass aside and pulled Rayna into a tight embrace, kissing her with such fervor, she could hardly breathe. When they finally separated, she gasped out, "Wait a minute! Let's not jump to conclusions. Remember, this is nothing more than conjecture until it can be proven."

Her statement dampened his enthusiasm. "You're right. You're right." For long seconds he stared ahead unseeing, lost in thought, before meeting her expectant gaze. "So, what's the next step? Should we contact the police?"

"That's one option. If we do that, they'll bring her in for questioning and may be able to break her story. But, you also don't want to take a chance on them panicking and skipping out."

Tyler's brows dipped in concern. "You think Scott would jump bond? No, I can't believe he'd do that."

"You know him better than I do. All I can tell you is I've seen it happen before."

He chewed on that for a moment. "Okay, let's assume that you're right. Why is Scott doing this? I can certainly understand him being in love, but to be willing to go to prison for her? It's so mind boggling, I can hardly grasp the concept."

"There's something else you don't know yet."

"What?"

"She's pregnant."

He stared at her in stunned silence, then whispered hoarsely, "I can't believe it. Scott is going to be a father?"

Rayna edged him a perceptive smile. "And you are going to be a grandfather."

"This is too much to absorb," he murmured with a note of wonder. "Well, who is this girl? Did you get her name?"

"I don't know her last name, but he called her Aubrey."

Tyler's mouth fell open. "What? Are you positive?"

Rayna sat upright, startled by his expression of horror. "Yes, I'm sure."

He covered his face with his hands. "Oh, my God. I can't believe this." He sat in silence for a few seconds before looking up. "I'd like to think it's just a coincidence, but...everything makes sense now."

"Tyler, what are you talking about?"

As if he hadn't heard her, he continued talking. "I knew it. I knew this would come back to haunt me someday. Even while it was happening, I was thinking to myself, I've become my father, and that's the last thing I ever wanted to do."

Rayna's heart contracted at his expression of abject misery. "Tyler, what is it?"

"Well, if my suspicions are correct, the girl you saw is Aubrey Miller. She's our housekeeper's daughter, and she and Scott have known each other since they were kids. Unfortunately, she turned out to be a real bad apple like her father. She's been in and out of trouble since she was...I don't know, twelve or thirteen."

"What kind of trouble?"

"You name it—shoplifting, vandalism, petty theft, and yes, drunk driving too. I did what I could to help at first, but Aubrey couldn't seem to stay on the right side of the law and I finally lost track of her."

"So, she's got priors," Rayna said, nodding sagely.

"Yeah. I guess it's been about three years ago now. I was away on one of my business trips when Camille called in hysterics one afternoon. She'd caught them together in his room. Mind you, he was only fifteen and she was nineteen at the time. Camille flipped out and took an overdose of sleeping pills. When she got home from the hospital, we did everything we could to discourage them from seeing each other again and..." he shook his head sadly, "I can't believe it, but history seems to be repeating itself. I actually made him promise me he wouldn't see her again."

He and Rayna exchanged a long solemn look as the personal significance of his statement registered. He averted his eyes, his throat clogged with emotion.

"I'm so sorry," Rayna murmured, her heart aching for him. She waited for a moment until he regained his composure before suggesting, "I almost hesitate to mention this, but it's something you'll have to face. If my suspicions are correct, it's very possible your grandchild will be born in jail."

Weighed down by the complexity of the situation, Tyler's shoulders sagged. Right on cue, Beauregarde jumped onto his lap and bumped his nose against him, as if he were trying to comfort him. Absently, Tyler stroked the cat's silky fur, then looked up to meet Rayna's empathetic eyes. "I know what Scott did was really stupid, but in an odd way, it's actually commendable that he's willing to make such a sacrifice and accept the consequences for a crime he didn't commit to protect his unborn child. If you think about it, he's far more courageous than I was at his age."

"Remember, even if everything we suspect is true, Scott is still not out of the woods, Tyler. He could be charged with Hindering the Prosecution. That's a class 5 felony."

"Man, is this ever complicated. So...what's the best way to handle this?"

Rayna pondered his question for a moment before answering. "I think you should confront Scott. You don't need to divulge how you found out. Tell him you hired a PI, whatever, but once he realizes that you know about Aubrey, I think he'll tell you the truth. If he does, then you'll have to convince him that it's best if she turns herself in to the authorities."

Tyler nodded in silence.

"Is Scott working tonight?"

"I think he's probably at the hotel with Camille."

She rose from the couch. "Well, then, as much as I'd like to keep you all to myself, I think the wisest thing to do would be to get over there as soon as possible and see if you can get this resolved. Pressure from both parents may be more effective, so since Camille is here, you may as well present a united front."

Appearing startled, Tyler asked, "Are you sure?"

She smiled. "I'm sure. Now go."

She accompanied him to the door and as he turned to leave, his eyes were warm with loving gratitude. "Counselor, you are one amazing lady."

CHAPTER FOURTEEN

Rayna stepped onto her balcony and lifted her face to the warm February sunlight. The wind chimes tinkled softly in a gentle breeze that carried the scent of blooming desert foliage and the promise of an early spring. As she gazed out across the rooftops to the majestic heights of the Catalina Mountains, which stood in stark relief against a cobalt blue sky, her throat tightened and her eyes misted with tears. It had been difficult, more difficult than she could have imagined, but after many sleepless nights and much soul-searching, she had come to terms with the fact that, if she were to realize her dream of being with Tyler, she must leave her home, her career, her wonderful friends, and the life she had carved out for herself in Tucson. It would not be easy. The idea of going back to South Carolina to start over was daunting.

It seemed impossible that two and a half weeks had passed since Tyler's unexpected return to Summersville on urgent business. He'd been rather vague about the reason, saying only that it required his personal attention. The knowledge that he would be flying in this afternoon made her stomach flutter with anticipation. Closing her eyes, she basked in the memory of the last night they'd spent together before he'd left Tucson. They had shared an intimate candlelit bubble bath, and afterwards slipped between the sheets, their skin still flushed from the warm perfumed water. Their passion for each other had been intense, their need for each other boundless. At dawn, they'd made love again before saying their goodbyes.

During his absence and in spite of their hectic schedules, they had made an effort to communicate as often as possible either by e-mail or phone, even though the calls were often brief. While he'd never failed to express how much he loved and missed her, it puzzled her that he'd been distant and oddly vague about when he might return to Tucson. It would have been easy to fall back into her old pattern of self-doubt and embrace the host of insecurities that had always ruled her emotions; easy to torture herself with the notion that his feelings for her had cooled. Instead she counseled herself to stay on a path of positive thinking. Most likely his preoccupation could be attributed to whatever problems he was experiencing in his business, combined with the ongoing personal and legal difficulties pertaining to Scott. But it remained troublesome to her that not once had he brought up the future of their relationship, nor had he mentioned whether any progress had been made concerning divorce proceedings with Camille.

She was glad, however, that Tyler had acted on her suggestion to confront Scott that same night that she'd shared her suspicions with him. He had left her condo and driven straight to the hotel. At first Scott had vehemently denied Tyler's allegations, but after continued pressure from him and Camille, Scott had finally acknowledged that it had been Aubrey driving the SUV the night of the accident. And yes, she had been drinking. Armed with his account, they went to the police department and Scott made a full report. Afterwards, accompanied by a police detective, the four of them had paid a surprise visit to Aubrey, who tearfully confessed. Out of deference to the young couple's dilemma, Tyler had magnanimously posted the high bond, and engaged another well-known attorney recommended by Rayna to handle her defense. He had told

171

Rayna that even though he didn't agree with Scott's choice of a mate, he vowed he would offer his support, because in his heart he recognized the sad fact that Scott's co-dependent behavior was a product of his dysfunctional family life. Whatever the outcome, he did not want to repeat the mistakes of his father.

The sensational turn of events had captured the attention of the statewide news media and Rayna couldn't help but laugh at the spectacle of Sheldon Freestone taking full advantage of the opportunity to promote himself, puffing and preening before the TV cameras like an overstuffed peacock. While the legal hurdles ahead for Aubrey remained substantial, the encouraging news that the mother and little girl were off the critical list helped diminish Tyler's anxiety by eliminating the possibility that the young woman might have been charged with manslaughter. However, much was unresolved and would remain that way for some time to come.

To Rayna's delight and surprise, Tyler had called her the previous evening to announce that he would be returning to Tucson earlier than originally expected. "I haven't forgotten that dinner I promised you," he said. "I hope you don't already have plans."

"Only to be with you. What time shall I be ready?"

"I'll pick you up at six o'clock sharp."

"What should I wear?"

"Something dressy."

"Dressy, huh? Are you going to tell me where we are going?"

Chuckling, he'd murmured, "Nope. You'll find out tomorrow night."

She longed to call Tracy and share the good news, but during their girl's night out last week, her friend hadn't done much to bolster her self-confidence. After three glasses of wine and much prompting, she'd finally told Tracy the entire story behind their rekindled romance. With a look of stunned amazement, Tracy had scolded, "Why didn't you ever tell me about all this before?"

"It was too painful to talk about."

"You poor baby," she'd commiserated, patting her hand sympathetically. "Well, you know me, I'm all for love and romance, and Tyler seems like a really nice guy, not to mention being a total hunk, but after all that's happened, what makes you think that you could ever really trust him again? And, even if he is sincere, do you really want to get yourself involved in his awful family situation?"

Rayna hated to hear her friend voice thoughts that she'd entertained herself. "I love him," she replied with a defensive shrug. "Granted, it's rather complicated,..."

"To say the least. Boy, talk about bringing baggage into a relationship. You two have got enough to fill up the cargo hold of a 747!"

"That's true, but I'm not a naive sixteen-year-old anymore. I'm going into this with my eyes wide open."

Tracy poured herself another glass of wine and shook her head sadly. "So, you're serious? You're going to give up a successful career that you worked your butt off for, your house, not to mention *me*, your very best friend in the world, and go live in some little jerkwater town with a guy who isn't even divorced yet?"

"Sounds like I've lost my mind, doesn't it?"

Tracy's eyes had softened with concern. "I sure hope you know what you're doing."

Miguel hadn't been any more encouraging when she'd mentioned her plans to him the following day. Dark brows set in a thoughtful frown, he'd cautioned, "Whoa, *Chica*, are you sure you've thought this through carefully?"

"I love him. I want to be with him. What else can I say?"

His steady gaze, while nonjudgmental, remained skeptical.

"Okay, that probably sounds simplistic. I know we have a few bumps in the road ahead of us, but whatever it is, I'm sure we can handle it."

"I just don't understand why, and I don't think it's right, that you have to make all the sacrifices. Why can't he come to you?"

"You don't realize all the ramifications. Brockwell Industries employs at least half the families in Summersville. There's no way he can ever leave there so...if we're going to be together, I have to go to him."

His face downcast, he'd muttered in a dejected voice, "Damn it, Rayna, I'm going to miss you."

"Oh, Miguel, I'm going to miss you too. More than you know."

The sudden drop in temperature as the sun retreated behind the western mountains brought Rayna out of her reverie with a start. There was no point in dwelling on the negative aspects of her situation. She glanced at her watch, realizing that Tyler would be arriving in less than an hour. Her stomach tingling with anticipation, she showered, then hurried to the closet to pull out the low-cut amethyst silk dress she'd been saving for a special occasion. Humming happily to herself, she carefully applied makeup and brushed her dark hair until it crackled with static electricity. She surveyed herself in the mirror with approval, jumping slightly when the phone rang. Inclined not to answer, she was prepared to let the call go to voice mail when she recognized Tyler's cell phone number on the caller ID. Grabbing the receiver, she exclaimed, "Hi, you're back!"

"Would I be speaking to the most beautiful woman in the entire world?" came Tyler's pleasant voice over the phone.

A delicious thrill ran though her body. "I don't know about that."

"Well, I do," he replied warmly. "I'm downstairs in the parking lot. Are you ready to go?"

"Yes, but don't you want to come up here for a few minutes? I thought maybe we'd have a glass of wine and kind of get reacquainted."

"Time for that later. I'll wait for you down here."

Before she could say anything else, he hung up abruptly. Bewildered, Rayna set the phone down. How strange. She thought he would be as anxious as she was to spend some time alone together before going to a public place. She picked up her jacket, stopped to pet Beauregarde goodbye and headed for the elevator, feeling uncertain.

Stepping outside into the cool night air, she gasped in shock at the sight of Tyler, nattily dressed in a black tux, standing beside a white stretch limousine. Bedazzled, she cried out, "What is this?" Moving to greet him, a pleasurable thrill rippled through her as his adoring gaze slowly caressed her from head to toe.

His dark eyes twinkling with mischief, he quipped, "The rental car agency offered it to me for only five dollars more than a regular sedan. I couldn't pass up a deal like that, now could I?"

"I should say not."

Bowing courteously, he took her hand to assist her inside the car and then climbed in beside her. After signaling to the driver, he drew her into his arms, murmuring, "God, I've missed you." He brought his lips down against hers in a slow, lingering kiss that banished all doubts and left her breathless with desire. When he finally pulled back, she stared up at him in query. "I don't know what's going on, but so far, I like it a lot."

"Good." He reached down and pulled a bottle of champagne from an iced silver bucket, then filled two long stemmed glasses. He clinked his glass to hers, all the while holding her with his hypnotic stare. "There's much more to come."

Smiling with delight, she snuggled next to him, inhaling the musky scent of his cologne, feeling the tension of the past few weeks seep from her body. He refilled her glass, and as she sipped the bubbly liquid, it slowly dawned on her that they were no longer in the city. Peering out the window, all she could see was the moonlit desert landscape and the dark outline of the mountains silhouetted against a starry sky. She turned back to meet his expectant gaze. "So, you're not going to tell me where we're going?"

"Patience, m'lady, you'll find out soon enough."

Giddy from the effects of the champagne, she surrendered once more to his heated embrace, kissing him with abandon, losing all sense of time and place until she felt the big car slow down and turn a corner. Hearing the crunch of gravel beneath the tires, she pulled back and gave him a puzzled look. "Where are we?"

His smile secretive, he pointed out the window.

Rayna's eyes widened as the car pulled up in front of John and Rose Dietermann's charming restaurant and stopped.

"What in the world...." Before she could complete her thought, the driver hopped out and held the door open for her and Tyler. When she stepped from the car, the front door of the little chalet flew open and the elderly couple came running out. "Welcome! Velcome!" they shouted in unison, rushing to greet them with wide smiles and hearty handshakes. "Good evenink, Mr. Brockwell." And to Rayna, "Hello! So vonderful to see you once again!"

"Hello again to you!" Rayna replied, still not quite sure what to make of everything. Turning back to Tyler, she exclaimed, "What a unique idea."

He smiled at her, his expression inscrutable. "Ah, but this is just the beginning." To the Dietermanns Tyler said, "We'll be ready in a few minutes," and then he linked arms with Rayna and led her along the narrow walkway bordered by dimly lit Malibu lights. When they rounded the corner to the *Biergarten*, Rayna stopped in her tracks, stunned by the transformation of the old place since her first visit. Gone were the crowded rows of picnic benches. In their place sat a solitary table draped in white linen, set for two. Adjacent to it, a cheery fire crackled in the natural stone fireplace. Overhead, rows of Japanese lanterns glowed softly and the air was perfumed with the heady scent of potted gardenias.

Enchanted, Rayna stood speechless for several seconds before meeting Tyler's warm gaze. "So…there's nobody here but the two of us?"

"It's a very private party."

"I don't know when you arranged this, but it is without a doubt, the most romantic thing anyone has ever done for me. It's nothing short of magical."

"I'm glad you approve," he said, pulling out her chair and seating her before pouring each of them a glass of Merlot. "Are you warm enough?" he inquired in a solicitous tone, taking a seat opposite her.

SYLVIA NOBEL

"Yes, I'm fine," she whispered, still unable to quite believe her good fortune.

"Are you hungry?"

"Starved."

They munched on toast points and goose liver pate', then Tyler held his glass aloft. "To us. And speaking of us, I apologize for not being more communicative these past few weeks. I've had a lot of details to work out, and I didn't want to get your hopes up concerning our future...."

"Wait," she cut in, reaching for his hand, lacing her fingers though his. "Before you say anything else, I have something to tell you."

He edged her a curious look. "What?"

She drew in a deep breath. "I'm not happy with the idea of having a long distance relationship and I don't want to waste another second of my life living alone. So...I've decided to move back to Summersville to be with you...if you'll have me."

Overwhelmed by the radiant glow of love reflected in her wide violet eyes, Tyler hesitated before he dared speak. "After I've caused you so much unhappiness, you would do that for me?"

"With no reservations whatsoever."

He swallowed hard and took a sip of wine before stating in a serious tone, "You know, I hate to bother you with business at such a moment," he said, reaching into his coat pocket, "but I was wondering if I could get your legal opinion on this contract I just signed. Could you tell me if you think it's binding?"

Taken aback by his sudden change of mood, Rayna frowned in surprise, but took the document and angled it towards the firelight. When she unfolded it, she drew in a sharp breath. "Oh, my God! Your divorce is final? When did this happen?"

"Camille finally agreed to the property settlement. I got the decree yesterday. I wanted to surprise you with it."

Unable to contain her joy, Rayna's eyes blurred with tears.

"There's something else. That day I first saw you in the courtroom, I vowed to myself that if I had to move heaven and earth to be with you, I would do it. It turns out that it was a lot simpler to move just me, so I met with a realtor this afternoon and signed a five-year lease for office space."

She stared at him in disbelief. "You're joking."

His face beamed with boyish excitement. "Nope. Tucson, Arizona is now the new corporate headquarters for Brockwell Industries. So, what do you think of that?"

Her voice trembling with emotion, Rayna said, "I think you are the most incredible man I have ever met."

Just then, the side door opened, and Rose Dietermann stepped out carrying a package wrapped in gold paper. She laid it in front of Rayna and gave Tyler a conspiratorial wink. "Let us know vhen you are ready for dinner."

"Thank you, Rose," Tyler said, favoring her with his engaging smile.

"What's this?" Rayna asked, so overcome by the chain of events, she could hardly think straight.

"Open it." His eyes twinkled with expectant pleasure.

Hands shaking with excitement, she peeled off the paper, and when she opened the package, she blinked in shock. Nestled in tissue paper lay the very same antique, hand-carved Reuge music box she'd bid on at the auction a month earlier. She ran her fingers over the smooth brass-inlaid wood. "This can't be! Someone else bought it. How did you...?"

"Tracy's mother was kind enough to track it down for me and apparently managed to keep it a secret from your friend as well."

Rayna's astonishment was compounded when she lifted the lid and the lilting strains of *Carolina Moon* resonated in her ears. "Oh, I love that old song."

Tyler's heart soared with elation. "I remember."

"But...the mechanism was broken. How did you find someone to fix it and substitute our song in such a short time?"

"It took a little doing," he said with a modest grin. "Now, there's something else." Without fanfare, he rose from his chair and knelt beside her chair, pulling a small velvet box from his pocket and pressing it into her hand "I should have done this twenty years ago."

Rayna's breath caught in her throat. Her heart pounding madly, she slowly opened the lid and stared in wonder at the sparkling diamond ring. Still speechless, she watched as he pulled the ring out of the box and slipped it on her trembling finger.

"My darling Rayna, I love you more than life itself. I've made a lot of mistakes in the past, but if you'll permit me, I plan to devote the rest of my life to making sure everyday from now on is a blue sky day. Will you do me the honor of becoming my wife?"

The words Rayna had waited so long to hear nourished her soul and brought joyous tears to her eyes. "Tyler, you know the answer is yes."

Not trusting his voice, Tyler rewound the music box and pushed to his feet, extending a hand to her. "May I have this dance?"

Rayna felt totally weightless as she accepted his outstretched hand and flowed into his arms. For a long moment, they stood absolutely still, locked in a gentle embrace, before Tyler began to lead her in a slow waltz to the delicate notes of the music. For Rayna, the sweet familiar tune resurrected the powerful, and unforgettable sensation of falling in love with him for the first time, and all the years seemed to melt away. His arms encircling her now felt like an uninterrupted, natural sequence to the vivid memories of their lost youth.

Tyler relished the feel of Rayna's body pressed against him, her arms wound around his neck. He touched his lips to her forehead, and when she raised her face to his, he said, "I do have just one more thing to ask you."

The look of tenderness emanating from his deep brown eyes made her wonder what else he could say that would make this evening more perfect. "What?"

"I know how hard you've worked and how much you value your career, but...how would you feel about starting our own family?"

As the significance of his words sunk in, Rayna thought her heart would burst with ecstasy. "Tyler, you'd better pinch me or I'll think this is all a dream."

"That's not a bad thing. I've been chasing this dream all my life," he whispered, tightening his hold on her. "Except this time, we're both in it."

DEADLY SANCTUARY

1

"Oh...my...God. What have I done?" I murmured aloud, staring transfixed at the barren desert valley below the roadside overlook. No way could this be my new home. No way. As I consulted the Arizona road map once again, a hostile brown wind charged up the steep cliff, whirling my hair into a tangle and filling my eyes with grit.

I began to regret my impulsive decision to take the newspaper job in Castle Valley. But, had there been any choice? All through the drive from Pennsylvania I had tortured myself with 'If onlys.' If only I hadn't been forced to a drier climate because of asthma. If only I hadn't lost my job at the *Philadelphia Inquirer*. If only Grant hadn't dumped me. If only, if only...

An odd snuffling, snorting sound made me whirl around and I froze in shock at the sight of six weird-looking creatures approximately the size of large dogs standing between me and the safety of my car.

A tentative step forward caused one of the grayish, bristle-coated animals to let out a bark and clatter its long, sharp fangs. What the devil were these things? They looked ferocious, like something out of a science fiction movie. Heart hammering, I shrank back against the stone retaining wall and edged a glance behind me to the sheer drop. There was no escape unless I suddenly developed the ability to fly.

A surge of panic contracted my chest. Stay calm, I urged myself. The last thing I needed right now was an asthma attack and to make matters worse, I realized that I'd left my inhaler in the car. If only a balky fuel pump hadn't detoured me off the freeway to Prescott for repairs, I wouldn't have even been in this godforsaken spot.

For some strange reason the beasts lost interest in me and dipped their heads to root among the dry weeds, flicking only an occasional wary look at me. Well, Kendall, what more can you do to screw up your life?

As I stood baking in the warm April sunlight, I cringed inwardly remembering how my well-meaning father had oversold my abilities to his old newspaper colleague, convincing him I was already a big time investigative reporter.

"Dad!" I'd whispered fiercely, "You know I was only in research."

He'd cupped his hand over the receiver. "It's not like you have a lot of options, Pumpkin. This place isn't far from Phoenix and he's got an opening. You talk to him." He set the phone against my ear.

"Hi," I said in a small voice. Morton Tuggs intimated that not only would my investigative background be a plus, he also needed someone he could trust. Three weeks prior, he stated, one of his reporters had mysteriously vanished without a trace.

That snagged my interest, but I felt a vague sense of foreboding when he seemed reluctant to answer any further questions on the phone.

"If you decide to take the job," he'd added gruffly, "we'll talk more when you arrive."

That would have been the time to confess my amateur status, but I'd said nothing.

The sound of an approaching vehicle pulled my attention to the road and a surge of relief washed over me when a tan pickup pulling a horse trailer roared into view. I waved my hand and the truck eased to a stop on the far side of the road. Two men got out. The driver, a tall lanky man wearing mirrored sunglasses, strolled toward me then stopped in his tracks and stared.

His older companion limped up behind him and gestured to my Volvo. "You got car trouble?"

I shook my head and pointed. Both men peered around the car, looked back at me, at each other, then broke into wide grins.

"Those pigs botherin' you, little lady?" asked the tall one, tipping the hat off his forehead, his mouth working a piece of gum. There was an unmistakable note of sarcasm in his voice.

Pigs? These hairy, sharp-toothed things were pigs? But why should that surprise me? They were like everything else I'd seen so far in this hot, dusty place: wild, prickly, and ugly.

He stepped forward, clapped his hands, and hollered, "Eeeeyaah!" The animals squealed and galloped away.

He turned back to me and swept the wide brimmed western hat from his head, revealing thick, blue-black hair. With exaggerated flair, he executed an elaborate bow, his smile mocking. "Always glad to assist a delicate damsel in distress." Even though I couldn't see his eyes, I could tell by the slow movement of his head that he was eyeing me from head to foot.

Damsel? Was that how I appeared? Delicate? Weak? Helpless? I squared my jaw. Was it just his macho behavior that irritated me, or the fact that I was burnt out on men altogether? A failed marriage and a broken engagement certainly entitled me to that.

The older man explained that the creatures were wild pigs called javelinas. "They look a mite fearsome, but won't usually hurt you unless you go after their young'uns." A friendly smile creased his sun-leathered face. By the look of their clothing, I gathered I'd come across some genuine Arizona cowboys.

"Should have guessed," the tall stranger said scornfully, pointing to my license plate. "She's a bird."

I bristled. "What do you mean?"

"Snowbird," the other man explained. "You know, tourist. Winter visitor. Folks who come here for the warm weather and then skedaddle."

"But," the contentious one cut in, "not before you people pollute our air, clog up our roads, use up our water, and trash the landscape."

"No offense intended, ma'am." The old cowboy shot a questioning glance at his friend.

But I did feel offended. Without stopping to think, the lie leaped to my tongue. "I am not a snowbird. For your information, I happen to be relocating to Castle Valley. I've accepted a very important...managerial position at their newspaper." I regretted my words immediately and wondered why I should even care what this arrogant man thought.

For a long minute they stared at me in silence, and then the tall cowboy grinned. "Well, now, is that a fact?"

A sharp ringing sound like metal striking metal, and a high whinny from the trailer got both men's immediate attention. "Come on, Jake," said the younger man, "we've wasted enough time. Let's get them back to the ranch." He reached the trailer in long strides, and I could hear him speak in a soothing voice to the horses.

I thanked Jake for his help, adding, "How do you stand him? He's the rudest man I've ever met."

His grin was sheepish. "Oh, don't pay any attention to Bradley. He doesn't mean any harm. Just doesn't like newcomers much, and you look a powerful lot like..."

His words faded as the ground suddenly swirled beneath me. I brushed a hand over my forehead as Jake stepped forward. Grabbing one arm, he led me to sit on a nearby rock in the shade of a scraggly tree. "You got water with you, little lady?" A look of concern deepened the creases around his eyes. "It's real dangerous to be out here without some. People dehydrate in a matter of hours. The desert, it ain't nothing to fool with."

I decided I'd rather die than admit I was an ignorant snowbird. "Yes, I have plenty in the car." He didn't need to know I had only a can of pop.

Bradley shouted from the truck. "Come on, Jake. Let's roll!"

I thanked Jake again for his kindness. He touched the brim of his hat murmuring, "Don't mention it," and limped away.

The dizzy spell behind me, I slumped into the ovenlike interior of my car and downed the last of the warm soda, jumping in alarm when a hand reached through the window on the passenger side.

Bradley dropped a thermos on the seat beside me. "You might need this."

I glared at him. "I'm fine. And anyway, I would have no way of returning this to you since it's highly unlikely we'll ever meet again." The haughty tone in my own voice surprised me.

The corner of his mouth lifted slightly. "It's a small world. You never know." Waving a final salute in my direction, he headed back to the truck. I felt like he'd given me the finger as they pulled away. His bumper sticker read, WELCOME TO ARIZONA. NOW GO HOME!

By the time I reached the sign telling me Castle Valley was fifteen miles away, I'd drunk half the water and was feeling rather foolish. The cowboy had been right after all.

As I slowed for a cattle guard, I noticed a girl alongside the road. It wasn't my habit to stop for hitchhikers, but when she frantically waved her hand, I pulled onto the shoulder and waited as she stooped to pick up her pack.

"Hey, thanks for the ride, lady." She plopped onto the seat beside me. "Jesus, it's hot out, ain't it?" I agreed and tried not to notice that she hadn't been within whistling distance of a shower for some time. "You headin' for Phoenix?"

"No. Just to the next town."

"Oh." A look of resignation flickered across her thin face. "No biggie. I'll get another ride. You care if I smoke?" She flipped a limp blond curl behind one ear.

"I'd rather you didn't," I answered, trying not to stare. Not only did she have a multitude of colorful tattoos, her left ear had been pierced eight or nine times. The array of earrings jingled when she moved.

"Hey, no problem." There was a hard edge about her. I noted her ragged jeans and faded T-shirt. What in the world was this girl doing out here in the middle of nowhere? Was she a runaway? She couldn't be more than sixteen. As we continued down the road, she spoke little, staring straight ahead with vacant green eyes.

I dragged my thoughts from the girl to examine my new surroundings. Morton Tuggs had told my father that Castle Valley was a beautiful place, and more healthful than Phoenix for me because it had no smog and was higher in elevation. My initial reaction was one of extreme disappointment. What a dinky town. It looked old and dilapidated, not at all what I'd imagined. A sign read: Population 5000. I wondered if that included the wildlife, as a prairie dog skipped across the road in front of me.

At least the sunset was gorgeous. It lit the sky in shades of red and orange, tinting the rock wall to the east a brilliant gold.

I stopped near the Greyhound Bus station, pressed a twenty dollar bill into the girl's hand, and suggested there might be a church or shelter where she could spend the night. She thanked me and got out, saying the money would come in handy since she was headed for Texas. As I watched her walk away, I suddenly felt lucky. Unlike her, I'd be staying at a cozy motel tonight and I had a job waiting.

The following day, I rose early, downed my asthma medication, and prayed the dry weather would cure me swiftly.

As I drove toward town, I wondered how I would survive in this place. The newspaper building looked just like the rest of the downtown area. Old and weatherbeaten.

7

The receptionist at the *Castle Valley Sun* greeted me with a dimpled smile, and introduced herself as Ginger King. She seemed delighted to hear that I might be joining the staff and took my elbow in a friendly manner while ushering me to Morton Tugg's office which was situated at the end of a short hallway.

I couldn't help but notice the smudged walls and frayed carpet as we reached the open doorway. From inside, a loud voice boomed, "The hell you say?" Hesitating, I turned questioning eyes to Ginger. "Don't fret none, sugar pie," she soothed, patting my hand. "His bark's a mite worse than his bite. Y'all can set yerself right there in front of his desk." Giggling, she gave me a little shove forward.

The bald, red-faced man seated at the incredibly cluttered desk waved me in while continuing to harangue whomever was at the other end of the phone.

The wooden chair wobbled on uneven legs when I sat. Clutching my purse in my lap, I surveyed the room. It was crowded and shabby, relieved only by bright travel posters adorning the walls. Then my gaze fell on Morton Tuggs.

"I wish I'd never let you talk me into this god-damned thing," he shouted, thumping the computer monitor. He didn't have hair one on the crown of his head, but as he listened intently, his fingers absently fluffed, then pressed flat, the tufts of fuzz perched over his ears like gray cotton balls. "I don't give a rat's ass what you say, just get the hell over here and fix it!" The phone dinged when he slammed down the receiver.

After a few breaths to compose himself, he threw me an apologetic smile. "Sorry about that." He reached out a welcoming hand. "So, you're Kendall O'Dell? Good to meet you. I see you got Bill's red hair. Quite a guy your dad. I guess he told you the story?" His brown eyes looked solemn, faraway. I took his hand, knowing he must be remembering the day my dad had saved his life when they'd both been foreign correspondents during the Vietnam War.

"It's nice to finally meet you too, Mr. Tuggs."

His other hand swiped impatiently at the air. "Tugg. Tugg. Everybody calls me Tugg." A hint of humor lit his face. "Except when they're calling me Tugboat behind my back."

I smiled, finally relaxing. We talked for a few minutes about what my routine assignments would be, the fact that his wife Mary had located several houses for me to look at and other general subjects.

During a lull in the conversation, I shifted uncomfortably in my chair. Was I wrong, or was Morton Tuggs deliberately avoiding the subject I most wanted to discuss? I cleared my throat. "You said on the phone you needed someone with my investigative background and someone you could trust. Do you want to tell me about this missing reporter?"

A look of anxiety etched his face. Instead of answering, he rose, shut the door, and returned to his desk where he laced his fingers in front of him. "I have to tell you that I've agonized for several weeks over how to handle this. It was my intent to have you look into it but, under the circumstances... perhaps it would be best not to pursue the matter further."

I eyed him suspiciously. He wasn't behaving very much like the hard-boiled newspaper editor my father had described. "A man doesn't vanish for no reason. What did the police report say?"

"There was a search. It was called off last week. I've pressed, but there doesn't seem much interest in pursuing the case. The official line coming down is that he probably just got bored with our little burg and skipped."

"What do you think?"

Tugg absentmindedly fluffed the patches of hair again. "John Dexter wasn't real well liked. He delighted in digging up dirt on people. Go through some of the back issues and you'll see what I mean. He had a knack for really pissing people off. But," he added, "even though he was sort of flaky at times, I can't believe he'd just up and go with no notice."

"So, I'll talk to the police and see what I can come up with. Perhaps there's a lead they've missed."

"No!"

I jumped as his fist crashed on the desk. Then, noting my obvious shock, he said, "I'm sorry. I didn't mean to startle you...it's just that...I'm not sure giving you this assignment would be the right thing to do."

Butterflies fluttered in my stomach. The major reason for my trip, resurrecting my aborted career, was fading before my eyes. "I'd appreciate a shot at this."

He swiveled in his chair and stared silently at the poster of Greece. After a minute he said quietly, "If you decide to work on this, it'll have to be strictly on the Q.T. Nobody else can know, and I'd caution you to be very, very careful."

His attitude disturbed me. It wasn't what he was saying, it was what he wasn't saying.

"Mr. Tuggs, Tugg..." I tried to keep the irritation from my voice. "You're going to have to level with me on this or I don't see how I can help. If you suspect foul play, which I gather you do, why aren't the police pursuing it, and why aren't you pushing for answers?"

As if struggling mightily with a difficult decision, he dropped his eyes and drummed his fingers on the desk. Abruptly, he pulled open a drawer and extracted a ragged piece of paper. He stared at it, chewing his lower lip. "John called me at home the afternoon before he disappeared. We were having a big get-together for my daughter and it was so noisy I was having trouble hearing him. I wish now I'd paid more attention 'cause I only remember bits and pieces of what he said." He sighed heavily. "Something about meeting a girl later. Her information would tie into what he'd been working on earlier in the week, and if he was right, it would blow the lid off this town." He stopped, rubbed his temples as if in pain, then continued. "He'd been going through some files over at the sheriff's office and told me he'd discovered something weird. I'm not sure if there's any connection, but, I found this in his desk a couple of days ago."

I studied the smudged paper he handed me. In between a profusion of doodling, I read the scattered phrases: Med records gone. Both cases. Dead teens. T prof...Connection? Possible cover up?

Before I could speak he added, "One more thing. And, this is a doozy, the part that's really got me boxed into a corner. The last thing he said before he hung up was, "'Whatever you do, don't mention this to Roy.'"

I looked up. "Who's Roy?"

The pained expression again. "My goddamned brother-in-law."

It was frustrating having to drag every word from him. "So?"

"He owns half this newspaper and...he's the sheriff."

2

I left Morton Tuggs' office, my head still reeling from his disturbing revelations, and trotted after Ginger, who'd been charged with familiarizing me with the layout. For the moment, I pushed the John Dexter puzzle to the back of my mind.

In the paper-littered production room, I shook hands with Harry, a big, burly man with coffee stains on his T-shirt, and then Rick, who peered at me owlishly through thick, horn-rimmed glasses. Lupe and Al, busy on the phones with classifieds, flashed preoccupied smiles. While Ginger prattled on, filling my head with endless personal statistics about each employee, I strained to maintain an expression of interest. The place was much smaller than I had imagined.

"And this here's your office." She gave a grand sweep of her hand.

Inwardly, I cringed in dismay at the sight of the dingy room crammed with several filing cabinets and three scarred desks topped with piles of clutter. Two smeary windows faced east overlooking the parking lot.

"Jim's out on assignment, but I see Tally's still here. He writes all the sports goodies." She nodded toward a man hunched over a desk in the far corner with his back to us, the phone cradled on his shoulder. A playful lilt edged her words as she sang out, "Hey, darlin'! Y'all turn 'round here and say 'howdy' to your new roommate."

Apparently absorbed on the phone, he didn't acknowledge us, so I told Ginger I'd meet him later. No sooner were the words spoken when he swiveled his chair around and stood to face us. Our eyes met, and my mouth sagged open as a jolt of recognition shot through me. It couldn't be! There in front of me clad in boots, jeans, and a checkered shirt, stood the tall, lanky cowboy from yesterday. The pig chaser.

Once again, he bowed deeply. "Bradley Talverson at your service...again, ma'am." His lips twisted in a wry smile as he motioned toward a tiny, metal desk. "I hope you'll find the...ah...accommodations here in the executive office to your liking."

With a chill of embarrassment, I remembered my fabricated tale of an important managerial position. So, that's why he'd acted the way he had. He must have thought I was a complete ass and I had no doubt my face was as red as it felt. The expression in his dark eyes challenged me to react. For what seemed an eternity, I wrestled with disbelief, regret and irritation. There seemed only one right thing to do. I laughed.

A look of surprise flitted over his lean face. "Well," he chuckled, widening his stance and folding his arms across his chest. "I'm glad to see you have a sense of humor."

Ginger regarded the two of us with astonishment. "Y'all know each other?"

"In a manner of speaking," he told her, and I couldn't help but notice his eyes brushing over me again. We parted on a handshake and my promise to return his thermos in the morning.

As I moved to the front door, I could tell by the look on Ginger's face that she was dying to know how we'd met. But I'd have to tell her some other time. Tugg had arranged for me to meet his wife, Mary at her realty office, and I was already late.

En route to the address, I thought about the rest of my conversation with Tugg. The newspaper had been owned by his wife's family for many years and her father had been editor up until four years ago when ill health forced him to retire. Under pressure, Tugg had given up a good position at the *Arizona Republic* in Phoenix and relocated to Castle Valley. He'd found the *Sun* in sorry shape and deeply in debt. A large infusion of cash was needed to keep it afloat, but no lending institutions were interested. Help had finally come from within the family. Roy Hollingsworth, recently married to Mary's twin sister, Faye, had advanced the money.

"You can see why I haven't been able to pursue this myself," Tugg had said glumly. "I'm between that rock and hard place you always hear about. Can you imagine what would happen if the paper accused Roy of dragging his feet on this investigation? If he pulls his financial support, we're sunk, not to mention that Mary would probably divorce me."

I asked him the best way to approach the subject with his brother-in-law.

SYLVIA NOBEL

"With caution," he warned. "Roy's not a man to piss
off. He's got a hard head, a short temper, and," Tugg
emphasized with a scowl, "he carries a gun. Just remember
that." Ushering me toward the door, he'd apologized for
placing me in such a delicate spot, but felt with my
background I'd be able to dig up something without being
discovered. Once again, the opportunity had come for me to
declare my amateur status, and, as before, I thought better
of it.

"Why don't you just hire a private detective or
something? That way there'd be no tie to the newspaper."

He looked weary. "I'm barely collecting a salary
now. Where would I get fifty bucks an hour to hire one?"

As I parked the car at the Castle Valley Realty
office, I had more than a few misgivings about my decision
to accept the position.

Mary Tuggs welcomed me with a beaming smile as I
stepped inside her office. "I'm so very glad to meet you."

At five foot eight, I towered over her tiny, round
frame. "My goodness, aren't you a sight! You remind me of
a young Katharine Hepburn."

That clinched it. I decided I liked Mary Tuggs a lot.
Outside again, I wondered if she'd need a leg up as we
approached her red Bronco. Somehow she scrambled into
the driver's seat without assistance. She showed me several
unremarkable dwellings nearby, renting for astronomical
prices, and then, noting my dismay, suggested a place
located five miles north of town. "Morty thought you might
like to at least look at it," she said, swinging onto the main
highway. "But I'm not sure you'll want to be so far from
town."

She told me that the three-bedroom, two bath house
was vacant because the elderly owner, Teresa Delgado, was

15

in a Phoenix nursing home recovering from a fall. Afraid of vandalism, she wanted Mary to find a trustworthy renter to occupy it until she returned. "It's been empty for a month now, so she's lowered the rent to get someone in there," she added.

"Sounds interesting," I replied, watching the cactus -covered landscape fly past. There wasn't another house in sight when we turned east and bounced along a rutted dirt road, leaving a plume of swirling dust in our wake.

"This is Lost Canyon Road," Mary informed me. "You'll be quite close to the Castle."

"Castle?"

She laughed and rolled her eyes. "Silly me. Of course you wouldn't know yet. That's Castle Rock," she said, pointing toward a mammoth, multi-colored rock formation. "It was named 'Castillo del Viento' by Spanish settlers. It means castle of the wind, isn't that pretty?"

I agreed and we'd just dipped into a dry sandy riverbed she called a 'wash' and were rounding a turn on the opposite hill, when she suddenly wrenched the wheel to the right. A black Mercedes with heavily tinted windows roared by leaving us in a choking cloud of dust.

My heart racing madly, I wheezed and reached for my inhaler.

"I'm so sorry!" White-faced, she pressed one hand to her chest. "What a maniac. He didn't even slow down." She shoved the truck into gear, grumbling, "That had to be someone from Serenity House. Except for the Hinkle Ranch a couple miles south of Tess's place, no one else lives out this way."

I took a few deep breaths and let the bitter-tasting medication seep slowly into my lungs. "What's Serenity House?"

She slanted me a sidelong glance. "Well...it's a mental hospital."

That captured my attention. "No kidding? What's it doing out here in the middle of the desert?"

"The property was cheap. It's on the site of an old Spanish monastery which was crumbling to ruins. Some developer restored it and tried to make a go of it as a health spa. When that failed, a psychiatrist named Isadore Price bought it about six years ago." She pursed her lips into a thin line. "That was probably his Mercedes."

"I hope he's a better doctor than he is a driver."

Mary frowned. "He's kind of a peculiar old bird. Keeps to himself mostly. I've only seen him a few times in town at a couple of social gatherings."

"Have there ever been any problems at this place?"

"To be honest, there was an incident right after they opened. One of the male patients escaped. He'd chopped up his family or something."

I shivered involuntarily.

"This town's never seen such excitement!" Her face became animated at the memory. "There was a huge manhunt, and everyone was pretty much on pins and needles until they found him. After that, a real high fence was built, and from what I've heard it's very well guarded. Nothing else has ever happened."

"How far is it from the Delgado place?"

"About two miles or so. And, of course, that's the whole idea of having it so secluded." She glanced at me again. "If it bothers you, I can turn around right now."

"No. I'd still like to see it."

"Okay," she said, steering onto another dirt road named Pajaro del Suspiro. Explaining it was Spanish for 'Weeping Bird,' she braked the truck in front of a brick-red

17

ranch-style wooden house surrounded by golden palo verde trees and saguaro cactus.

I got out and took a sniff of the warm, pristine air. Yep. Just what the doctor ordered. I followed Mary up the stone walkway and when she pointed to the giant rock formation, I stopped in amazement. It did resemble a castle and the effect was breathtaking.

While she fiddled with the door key, I listened to the lonesome keening of the wind and wondered if I could stand to live in such isolation. My misgivings faded as she led me through the spacious interior, decorated in bright Southwestern colors and heavy, Spanish-style furniture. It was a gigantic improvement over the cramped apartment I'd just left in Philadelphia, and far cheaper. I expressed surprise that she'd had difficulty keeping it rented.

"The trouble is," Mary said, showing me through the sunny kitchen, "most renters want a signed lease, and Tess won't have it because she wants the freedom to return on short notice. That's the minus, but," she added with a cheery smile, "here's a plus. The last tenants left in such a hurry, I never got a chance to refund their deposit. So, if you decide to take it, the first month would be free."

"I like the free part, but, what does the 'left in a hurry' part mean?"

Mary opened the front door. "They called me out of the blue late one night, and announced they were leaving right then and there."

"Why?"

There was no mistaking her tone of skepticism. "Tess certainly never mentioned it, but…they swore this place was haunted."

3

Fascinated by Mary's intriguing remark, I chose to put aside my misgivings and move in. The proliferation of insects that trooped in and out of the Delgado house the first few days bothered me more than the supposed phantom. I'd always considered myself fairly brave for a woman, having no particular fear of snakes, mice, or bats. But, when it came to insects, spiders especially, I turned into a shivering coward. There seemed to be an abundance of the eight legged creatures about, plus scorpions, centipedes, and humongous roaches. At my request, Mary sent the exterminator.

On his second visit in three days, overall clad, grizzle-faced, Lloyd "Skeeter" Jenkins of the Bugs-Be-Gone Exterminating Company, told me all I needed to know, and more, about the insects and rodents indigenous to the great state of Arizona.

"Now I kin git rid o' them pesky mice fer ya, an' the powder I'll lay down'll keep them centipedes and scorpions on their toes, so to speak. Spiders is something else again.

Them suckers kin walk right over the stuff with them long legs o' theirs."

He left me with the sage advice to "never put yer shoes on in the mornin' till you've whopped 'em good. There's no tellin' what kinda critter mighta moved in an' set up housekeepin' durin' the night."

I wondered if I'd ever get used to the bugs, the dust, and the scalding sun. The calendar said it was still April but I could have sworn spring had been canceled and we'd gone right into summer as it was already in the 90's. My asthma had improved, but I was miserably hot.

"Don't you worry, sugar," Ginger had soothed hearing my complaint, "as soon as your blood thins, y'all will git used to it." I wasn't sure I wanted my blood to thin.

My first week on the job was an exercise in frustration and adaptation. The *Sun*, a sixteen page tabloid, was published only twice weekly, Wednesdays and Saturdays. I sorely missed the daily deadlines, the lively newsroom chatter, and stimulation of the big city. I knew I couldn't go back to damp, cool Pennsylvania and face a life of being incapacitated, yet I didn't want to stay either.

My other co-worker—young, blond, brash and not overly bright Jim Sykes—didn't sympathize with my position. He grabbed all the interesting assignments while I got the leftovers. If I had to cover one more banquet, Ladies Club function, or write one more article about who was visiting whom from out of town, I felt I'd go nuts.

After banging my knee on the narrow desk for the third time that morning, I grumbled, "I hate this damn thing."

Bradley Talverson swiveled around at my remark, and taunted me with a crooked grin. "Welcome to the club. We all started at the rookie desk. Now it's your turn."

"Yeah," young Sykes joined in. "Now that Johnny boy's split, you're low man on the totem pole."

I glanced swiftly from one to the other. Neither man seemed particularly disturbed by his disappearance, and I reminded myself again that even they could not know of my secret assignment. I phrased my question carefully, trying to sound indifferent. "Oh, yeah. What was he like? John Dexter, I mean?"

Bradley's eyes narrowed. "All hat and no cattle."

I raised an eyebrow. "Come again?"

"He was a pain in the ass. Interested only in trash journalism."

"But he was real popular with the ladies. Married or single, right Tally?" Jim's eyes gleamed wickedly.

I knew there was some significance to the remark by the deadly expression on Bradley's face before he turned his back to us. His constant mood swings puzzled me. Sometimes he was cordial and friendly. At other times, withdrawn, angry almost, as if he were struggling with some inner demon. More than once, I'd caught him looking at me with an unreadable expression in his dark eyes.

Anxious to pursue the subject of John Dexter, I had just formulated my next question when Ginger stuck her head in the doorway. "Come on, sugar, let's shake it. Time for lunch."

Damn! If only she had waited five minutes. Bradley and Jim resumed their work; my chance for more questions gone for now.

As we walked the three blocks to the Iron Skillet, I silently thanked God for Ginger King who'd unabashedly inserted herself into the vacant slot in my life marked: friend. Short and round with light brown hair and sparkling

21

ginger-colored eyes, she bubbled over with good humor. She was also a hopeless gossip. Endearing, but hopeless.

Three days earlier, during our first lunch together, she'd shrieked with laughter when I recounted my story of meeting Bradley, whose close friends called him Tally, she informed me. I learned about her family, her life in Texas, and her heartfelt desire to settle down and have children.

"How old are you, sugar?"

"Twenty-eight."

"Well, y'all still have some time. I'm gonna be thirty-three next month, and eligible men in this town are scarcer than hen's teeth."

Mingled between anecdotes about the good citizens of Castle Valley, she skillfully extracted large chunks of my background.

"I got married right after college, but it barely lasted two years."

"Oh, that's a shame." For a few seconds her expression was sympathetic, then it turned impish. "So, what happened? He beat ya? Chase other women? Was he gay?"

I laughed. "I think you've been watching too many talk shows. Sorry to disappoint you, but it was nothing so dramatic. I'd been working at my dad's newspaper since I could read and could do every job there practically in my sleep.

"I was restless, ready to move on and my husband was studying to be a pharmacist. His plans included us staying in Spring Hill, complete with picket fence and a dozen kids. Mine didn't. Neither of us could change, so we parted friends. He got the dog, and I took my maiden name back."

Throughout the remainder of the meal, she'd pressed me for further details, and it was amusing to hear some of the things I'd told her, repeated by other staff members the following day. Some details were embellished almost beyond recognition.

With that in mind now, as we entered the restaurant and slid into the red vinyl booth, I vowed to talk less of myself and concentrate on extracting information from her.

"Oh, lookee here," she cried, eyeing the menu with regret. "Chicken and dumplin's. And me on a stupid diet again."

"Go ahead and have it if you want it."

She drew back in mock horror. "Easy for you to say, being skinny as a rail. Food don't go to my stomach, darlin'. Everything goes right here," she complained, patting her hips.

We were both giggling when a chestnut-haired woman interrupted, asking for our order. "Oh, Lucy," Ginger gushed, a sly expression stealing over her features, "this here's Kendall O'Dell. Kendall, this here's Lucinda Johns. She and her Aunt Polly own this place."

When I told her how much I'd enjoyed the previous lunch, she smiled and thanked me. As she took our orders, I couldn't help but notice her enormous bustline. It made me feel positively flat.

"Kendall's our new gal on the beat over yonder at the paper. Ain't that nice?" The syrupy tone of Ginger's voice surprised me.

Curious, I glanced at her, then back to Lucinda in time to see her smile shrink. "I see. Congratulations." She cast a speculative glance at me before turning away.

A mischievous light gleamed in Ginger's eyes. "Okay," I demanded, "what was that little scene all about?

23

You might as well have told her I have AIDS by the way she acted."

"I just wanted to see if she'd act jealous."

"Jealous of whom?"

She studied her fingertips. "You."

"Me? Why?"

"'Cause she's had her eye on Tally since grade school. Her knowing y'all are there practically sitting in his lap all day'll keep her on her toes."

"I'm surprised at you. That was downright catty."

"I can't help myself."

"Well, she needn't worry. I'm totally burnt out on the male sex at this moment."

She cocked her head in question, so I told her the barest details about my shattered romance with Grant Jamerson, glossing over most of the painful details. "It was for the best, however. He'd have made a lousy husband."

As the noisy lunch crowd filled the room, I watched Lucinda and another waitress scurry from table to table. Five minutes later, she set the plates down in front of us without a word and managed the barest of smiles before rushing away.

I shook my head sadly. "Shame on you, Ginger. I've only been here nine days, and already I have a mortal enemy."

"Oh, flapdoodle. She'd have found out about y'all eventually any hoot. She keeps pretty close tabs on him."

I dug into my tuna salad. "So, they're an item?"

"If Tally was willing, she'd drag him to the preacher tomorrow. He's quite a catch y'know."

Ignoring her implication, I buttered a roll and yawned my disinterest. "To each his own, I guess."

"A gal could do worse."

SYLVIA NOBEL

I stopped eating. "Forget it, Ginger. I don't mean to sound condescending, but I can do better than a hired ranch hand."

She choked on her sandwich. "Ranch hand! Didn't anybody tell you? He and his family own the Starfire. It's one of the biggest dang cattle ranches in the state."

I felt like my chin was going to hit the table. The sparkle in Ginger's eyes reflected her enjoyment.

"Well, what's he doing working at that two bit...I mean at the paper?"

"He ain't been there but two years. He needed to git his mind off of what happened, I guess." A dreamy look came over her face. "It musta pert near stopped his heart when he laid eyes on you the first time."

"Why?"

"With all that flaming red hair? He's gotta be thinking of his wife, Stephanie."

I'm sure my face looked incredulous. "If he's married, why should Lucinda be jealous of me?"

"He ain't married no more. Stephanie's dead as a doornail. Rode out one stormy night on one of them prize appaloosa horses of his and got throwed off. Died of a broken neck, she did." It was obvious by the satisfied gleam in her eyes that she was relishing every word.

"No kidding?"

"Yep. But that ain't the half of it." She lowered her voice. "Now, I ain't one for carryin' tales, but some folks 'round here didn't think it was no accident, including our very own John Dexter."

"Really? And, what did he think?"

"That Tally killed her."

25

4

Ginger's remark blew me away. While the disclosure about Bradley was shocking, more intriguing yet was John Dexter's connection.

"Okay, you've got my undivided attention. Why did he suspect Bradley had anything to do with her death?"

She opened her mouth to speak when a loud voice from across the room cut her off. I turned to see Lucinda blocking the exit of a rather disheveled looking teen-ager clad in ragged jeans and tank top.

"This ain't a charity dining room. I'm sick to death of you free loaders jumping off the bus and coming in here to order up a meal you can't pay for!" She hustled the girl out the door. "You want a free meal, get your butt to the shelter three blocks over."

The teen cast a spiteful glance at Lucinda before slinking away, and I couldn't help but think of the pathetic young girl I'd picked up last week.

For a few seconds, the room was bathed in silence, and then one grizzled customer drawled, "Aw, Lucy. Now what'd you go an' do that for? She looked real pitiful, like a starved pup. You're not gonna go broke sharin' a sandwich with the kid." That brought a hoot of laughter from the man's companions.

Lucinda fixed him with a formidable glare. "You mind your own business, Elwood. I wouldn't care if it was just once in a while, but this is getting real old. It seems like every ragamuffin runaway in the country makes a beeline for my place. I can't afford to feed all of them. Let that Phillips woman do her job." With that she dusted her hands together and marched behind the counter.

"Poor little things," Ginger sighed, her expression troubled. "My sister Bonnie was showing me a magazine article just last week. They're called throwaway kids." Her voice got lower, more confidential. "As young as eleven or twelve they're turning tricks for food and money. Ain't that jest shameful?"

"Awful. What shelter is Lucinda talking about?"

In between bites of her sandwich, she told me about the Desert Harbor Shelter located in a "big ol'" house on Tumbleweed, and run by a woman named Claudia Phillips. "I heard tell the place operates on a shoestring. She can't do a whole lot but give them kids some food and clothes and a place to stay a spell." Then, with an ominous tone, she added, "Them are the lucky ones. Some of them little gals just plum vanish. Poof!"

"Vanish?"

"White slave traders."

"What are you talking about?"

"It was in all the papers. This gang was taking blue-eyed blonde gals and selling 'em to them people over yonder for their harems or some such thing."

"Oh, Ginger, get real."

"I swear on my mama's Bible! And then there was that bunch in Mexico snatching 'em up for human sacrifices."

Impatient to return to the previous subject, I steered the conversation back to John Dexter's suspicions about Bradley.

"Oh, yeah. Well, as I was sayin'..." She glanced at her watch and wailed, "Good Lord, it's almost one o'clock. Tugg's gonna have my fanny in a crack if I'm late again! I gotta scoot."

Twice now in two hours I'd let myself get sidetracked. "Wait a minute! You can't just drop a bombshell like that and then leave me hanging."

"Sorry, sugar. Lookee here. Why don't y'all come on over to supper tomorrow night? I'll rustle up a pot of my famous Texas chili, some homemade cornbread, and fill in the rest."

"Okay."

She scribbled her address on a napkin and bolted out the door.

Aware that I had twenty minutes to kill before covering another terminally boring meeting at City Hall, I stepped outside, squinting into the glaring sunlight. I'd walked only a few feet from the door when one of Ginger's remarks struck me. Had I been so busy concentrating on what John Dexter had to do with Bradley's wife that I'd missed something important? Plopping down on the nearby shaded bus bench I pulled out the note Tugg had given me and read it again, zeroing in on the phrase, "dead teens."

I flipped open my notepad. In the center of the page, I drew a circle, wrote John Dexter's name in the middle, and then extended lines outward like bicycle spokes. On each line I placed one of the statements in the note, then leaned back against the hard wooden backrest to study it, only vaguely aware of people and traffic.

Was I way off base or could there be some connection between the dead teens and the runaways Ginger spoke of? Dexter had referred to something odd in some files at the sheriff's office. Were they the same ones he'd mentioned in the note?

I blew out a long breath. Obviously, I had my work cut out for me. On a new page, I made a note to go through past issues of the *Sun* and study the stories Dexter had written on the two cases. Step two would be the doozy; tactfully asking to see the files without agitating Roy Hollingsworth whom I'd finally met for the first time the previous Friday. Tugg had assigned me to cover the police blotter, or log as they called it. That would put me in the sheriff's office at least once a week.

I'd been surprised when I met Roy. From Tugg's description, I had expected to encounter a thoroughly uncooperative, disagreeable, perhaps even dangerous man. He appeared to be none of those, greeting me with a wide smile and a neighborly handshake. Standing well over six feet tall, his substantial stomach protruding over a gigantic turquoise belt buckle, he looked less like an adversary than he did a big, friendly bear. In uniform.

As we chatted, I couldn't help but stare at his curious eyebrows. They were light blonde, very fuzzy, and perched over his silver blue eyes like two giant caterpillars. I hid my surprise when he brought up the subject of John Dexter.

"Morty's been real unhappy with me over our manhunt for John Dexter, but as I tried to tell him, we can't produce the man out of thin air. Me and Deputy Potts, along with members of the sheriff's posse and other law enforcement agencies, combed this area for weeks and couldn't find a trace of him." Shrugging his aggravation, he added, "It's been real frustrating for me, too."

He was very convincing. I began to wonder if Tugg was on the wrong track. "I'm sure we'll hear from him sooner or later. When did you last see him?"

"Julie," he shouted. "Pull the file on John Dexter for me." Moments later, a slender, dark-haired girl appeared from another room and handed him a folder. The sheriff rifled through it as Julie and I exchanged introductions.

"He disappeared on March 29th, and I may have been the last person in town to see him. The reason I know that is because I wrote him a speeding ticket that day."

Tugg hadn't told me that. "Where did you ticket him?"

"Heading south on 89 toward Phoenix. He seemed real nervous when I stopped him. Agitated. He was...well, let's say, verbally abusive, but for John that wasn't out of character." He smiled wryly. "So you see, I don't think anything unusual happened to John. I think he had something else going. Why he didn't give Morty notice, I don't know." When he frowned, the two blond caterpillars fused together into one.

While he shuffled papers into the file, I decided either he was being quite up front with me or he was a remarkably good actor. He'd ushered me to the door, inviting me to come anytime or call him if I had any questions. Because he'd been so damned likable, it would make my job all the harder.

A car backfire jolted me back to the present. I closed the notebook and rose stiffly from the bus bench. The meeting ran for over two hours, and it was late afternoon when I returned to the newspaper office. Ginger greeted me with a smile reminding me again of dinner the following evening. I hauled out three boxes of back issues of the paper to take home with me.

The wind was blowing across the desert floor, whipping up funnels of yellow dust when I reached the house. Before going inside, I paused as I always did to admire the spectacle of Castle Rock. Ever changeable, depending on the angle of the sun, it glowed in shades of peach and burnished copper.

After an early dinner, I phoned my parents. They seemed pleased I was settling in. Dad asked about my job, Morton Tuggs, and my asthma. With forced enthusiasm, I told them about my new life and promised to call them again soon. As I hung up the phone, a sharp pang of homesickness enveloped me. To ward off the blues, I turned up the television and cleaned the kitchen.

Still filled with restless energy, I went outside to sweep the walkway and water the small front garden filled with a bright orange sea of desert poppies. The sound of a vehicle made me look up. The black Mercedes I'd seen the first day purred down Lost Canyon Road followed by a white van. Was that perhaps my nearest neighbor, Dr. Price? I'd been meaning to check out Serenity House for days now, but hadn't had the time. I decided a nice long walk would do me good. Mary Tuggs had said it was about two miles away, so I should be back before dark.

It was so quiet I could hear my tennis shoes crunching on the rocky road. Except for the birds and an occasional gust of wind, nothing disturbed the silence.

When I reached a fork in the road, I chose the left which looked well traveled. The right fork, overgrown with tall grass and tumbleweeds, snaked off into the desert. I slowed my footsteps as I approached a large sign with bold

31

red letters announcing: DANGER! NO UNAUTHORIZED
PERSONNEL BEYOND THIS POINT.

The high fence topped with jagged coils of razor
wire looked ominous, but in a way it made me feel secure to
know it was there. For a fleeting second, visions of violent
ax-wielding mental patients flashed through my mind like
scenes from a cheap horror movie. "Don't be stupid," I
muttered under my breath. I'd read that many of the new
drugs did an excellent job of subduing patients.

I peered through the chain-link fence. Enclosed
inside a second fence I spotted the top of an ancient bell
tower. Patches of red tile roofs and white stucco buildings
were visible among the groves of palms and cottonwood
trees. It looked quite peaceful and not at all threatening.

Then, seemingly from out of nowhere, two
enormous Dobermans rushed to the fence, eyes gleaming,
teeth snapping, their throaty barks echoing through the
stillness. My heart pounded as I jumped back. Without
hesitation, I retreated. All during the walk home, the
memory of the dogs' snarling faces kept me in a state of
watchful anxiety.

Sometime during the night, the wind kicked up
again. It whistled around under the eaves and rattled the
windows. For hours, I thrashed about restlessly. When I
finally did fall into a deep sleep I kept having the same
annoying dream over and over. A voice kept calling for me
to get out. "Get out. Get out."

The persistent phrase was so irritating, I finally
opened my eyes. Then I heard it again. Was I awake or still
dreaming?

"Get out!" The voice was quite distinct that time.
This was no dream! Pulse racing, I sat bolt upright in bed

and stared at the partially open arcadia door. "Who's out there?"

Besides the murmur of the wind rustling through the trees, I thought I heard footsteps disappearing into the distance.